CW01269679

THE SHADOW OF TWO SUNS

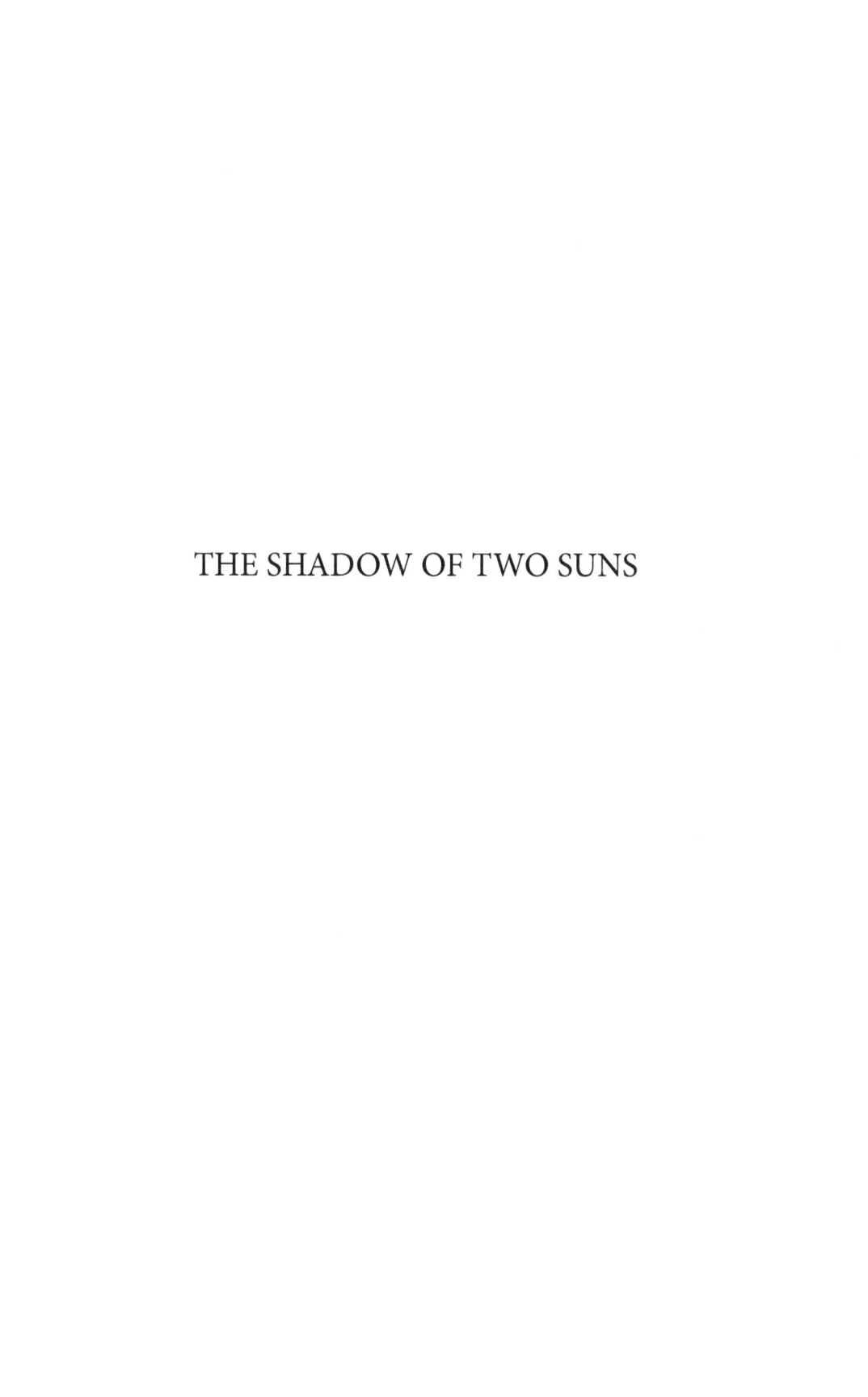

THE SHADOW OF TWO SUNS

A MERGING WORLDS BOOK

PETER A. HEASLEY

This book is a work of fiction. Any references to historical events, real people, or real places are used fictitiously. Other names, characters, places, and events are products of the author's imagination, and any resemblance to actual events or places or persons, living or dead, is entirely coincidental.

Copyright © 2024 by Peter A. Heasley

All rights reserved, including the right to reproduce this book or portions thereof in any form whatsoever except as quotations in book reviews.

First hardcover edition December 2024

On the cover:
  "Jupiter Showcases Auroras, Hazes (NIRCam Closeup)." Original image by NASA, ESA, Jupiter ERS Team; image processing by Judy Schmidt, inverted by Peter A. Heasley.

ISBN 979-8-9867574-9-0 (hardcover)

peteraheasley.com

For all in prison, whatever its shape

"For some time we had been tormented by doubts as to who was a monster and who wasn't, but that too could be considered long settled: all of us who existed were non-monsters, while the monsters were all those who could exist and didn't, because the succession of causes and effects had clearly favored us, the non-monsters, rather than them."
—Italo Calvino

PART ONE

COMMUTE

1

The death house was quieter than I had expected. There was only so much attention a man needed during the day, even on his last day, and the tie-down team had not passed the time talking to me. They had given me instructions when I had arrived yesterday and left me alone in this cell. The guards wanted nothing to do with me. I could understand that.

The warden, though, had insisted I keep my sketchbook, and that had helped me through the past twenty hours of silence. The stillness had made it hard to sleep last night. The slightest jingling of a guard's keys would send me waking. So, I drew. The rubbing of pencil on paper along with rustle of fabric, jumpsuit against bedclothes, had somehow soothed me, lulled me back to sleep, or at least half sleep, several times. I woke up this morning with a dozen unfinished drawings: of my mother and the smile that had always calmed me down; of Mireille, about whom I should have been wasting no more time thinking; of my toes, the last thing I would see in this life.

The empty tray of my last meal sat next to my sketchbook on the metal desk. It had come through a slot in the cell door half an hour ago. "Mac 'n' cheese," the guard had called out, like a line order cook to a waitress. That had been my request. It was practically all my mother had fed me as a child, from boxes in the kitchen cabinet. What I had to show for it was five-foot-six-inches of bone and tendons. Maybe she should have made me tuna sandwiches, too. After twenty-one years of life, I would not have much meat to give back to Mother Earth after my execution. They would probably cremate me and scatter my crushed bones in the wind, anyway.

I looked around the room. A single-size mattress sat on a metal frame in the corner, its sheets and blanket neatly tucked. That had been me. If I was going to have anything in this life, I was going to take care of it. The concrete block walls were painted cream. The floor was checkered tiles of dark and light brown. Add a metal toilet, a metal sink, and the metal desk at which I sat, and that was it. My last home on Earth.

I turned around to sketch. I was not afraid to think about what was coming. There was just not much about which to think. I had no imagination for the afterlife, no fear of God or hell, and just assumed my consciousness would turn off if I even continued to exist anywhere. If my mother were still alive, or if I had ever mattered to anyone other than the hot minute I had known Mireille, I might have thought more of myself and what my existence meant to the universe. The more I meant to others, the more I might have feared death. But the impression some people made in this world was nothing more than the whiff of piss in an alley, easily washed away.

I heard footsteps coming up the corridor. I let out a long, stowed breath.

Two, maybe three bodies. A fat man in sneakers: a guard. The echoed clacking of hard-soled dress shoes: the warden. Make that two pairs of dress shoes. No, three, along with the striking of a cane: a mystery.

The fat guard showed up first. He looked right at me, confused and happy, as he turned the key. The guy had never smiled at me before, and I was not sure why he was doing so now. I still had an hour before he took me away.

The warden entered my cell, crossed his arms, and smirked but said nothing.

A lawyer followed, holding a leather portfolio in his hand.

A tall man with the cane stood back in the corridor.

The lawyer unzipped his portfolio, pulled out a manila folder, and said, "Shelton Keyes?"

"You putting someone else to death today?" I said. I did not know this lawyer.

"Now, Keyes," the warden said, "these men might be able to offer you an opportunity."

"What for?" I said.

The warden turned to the fat guard and said, "We'll call you when we're done."

When the guard's footsteps faded away, the lawyer said, "Mr. Keyes, I represent the International Office of Special Science. Do you know what that is?"

I pulled my head back and tried not to grin. Some said the IOSS operated above world governments, above Trans Sahara, even above the United States. "Yeah. Spook city."

He grimaced. "We are scientists seeking answers to all that has befallen Earth in the past eighty years so that we can find a way forward for humanity."

That sounded scripted. "What does that got to do with me?"

"Mr. Keyes," the lawyer said, obviously reading from my jacket in the manila folder, "you did not appeal conviction or sentencing."

"Correct."

"Any reason why?"

"I killed a cop. You don't get to live long after that, no matter where you are. I'm surprised his partner didn't gun me down when he had the chance."

The warden said, "Because Officer Hernandez is a cool-headed professional. But I don't think these gentlemen are here to talk about the past. Are you?"

"No, we're not," the lawyer said. "We need you for the future."

"You want a body to experiment on?" I said. "I don't got much to offer."

The IOSS lawyer laughed. "I think if we opened you up, Mr. Keyes, we'd only find macaroni, cheese, and anger."

"Oh, this lawyer's got a sense of humor," I said to the warden, pointing at the man. "And a sense of smell, too. Here. There's a little left in the tray. Y'all can't make it like Mom did."

As I turned my gaze back to the lawyer, I caught the eyes of the man with the cane, who stood still in the corridor. Those blue eyes were not laughing. I was about to make some comment about that man, too, but those blazing blue eyes somehow pinned me down.

"Alright. Tell me," I said. "What are y'all here for?"

"We want to transfer you to an experimental prison."

I looked at the ceiling. It was painted concrete. I closed my eyes, sighed, and looked back down. "How…experimental?"

"In the best-case scenario, it would be a self-governing situation, a de facto life sentence."

I rubbed the back of my neck. "Governed by other inmates?"

"In the best-case scenario."

That could not possibly be anyone's ideal situation, except for the toughest guys in prison. "And in the worst?"

"You are under a sentence of death, which will not officially have been commuted."

I turned my chair to face the lawyer. "I get it. There's a good chance I die in your experimental prison. And if not, I've got to live with other inmates and their rules? No way. Listen," I held my left wrist to my eye, reading a watch that was not there, "in one hour, I get killed anyway, and no more hassle after that. No more looking over my shoulder. Besides, who's to say the dead cop's buddies don't track me down? Then your efforts are wasted."

The lawyer looked at the warden and then at the man in the corridor. To me, he said, "Mr. Keyes, I guarantee that you will be out of reach of this world's requital."

"There's always payback in this world," I said.

"That much is true," the lawyer said.

I held my arms stiffly on my legs, pinning my back

against the frame of the metal chair. Neither the lawyer nor the warden nor the man in the corridor said anything. I was supposed to understand something they were saying. I did not.

"No disrespect to the warden here, but why don't you guys speak clearly?" I said.

The blue-eyed man in the corridor cleared his throat. He began hobbling on his cane into the cell and said, "Let me have a moment."

The IOSS lawyer turned aside, and I saw the tall man fully for the first time. He was a chaplain. But chaplains were either pudgy, red-cheeked white guys who wanted you to share your feelings or Black guys in ill-fitting suits who called you "brother" and told you they had once been there, too, knew exactly how you were feeling. This chaplain wore a button-down, black dress that ran to the floor, and the taut skin of his face shined more like polished bronze than the color of any earthly race. His blue eyes, I swore, glowed, and if not for the way he cleared his throat again as he sat on the bed across from me, I would have thought he was a walking statue. The head of his cane was a brass owl.

"We'll be just a minute," the chaplain said.

The warden and the lawyer walked into the corridor but not too far away.

I turned in my chair to face the chaplain sitting on the bed.

The chaplain looked at my bare feet and at the tattoos I had on each hand but did not comment on any of that.

"Why didn't you make him kill you?" he said.

This was not the question I expected a chaplain to ask

first. The truth was, I had been asking myself the same question for the past ten months.

"You still had the gun in your hand, Shelton. You knew you had killed Officer Ling. You knew it was a death sentence no matter what. Why not get it over with back then? Just pull the gun toward Officer Hernandez and save yourself the trouble of the past year?"

"I don't mean no disrespect, Mr. Chaplain, but I don't see what this has got to do with science experiments. You're here to convince me to do something."

"That's fair, Shelton. So, let me ask you about the crossed keys tattooed on your right hand."

"Shelton Keyes is my name. Skeleton keys on my hand. Simple as that."

"In my tradition, Shelton, the crossed keys are a sign of authority, given to Saint Peter. *Amen I say to you, whatsoever you shall bind upon earth, shall be bound also in heaven; and whatsoever you shall loose upon earth, shall be loosed also in heaven.* But you're a collector by trade. You've opened the doors of a lot of abandoned homes and offices in this world without needing keys. You've brought an old world to life for people who have forgotten it and people who have never known it."

I was a collector. I went back to those places humans had left behind after the Earth had decided it wanted a heavy winter circling the upper latitudes every eighteen years and salvaged what I could for those who had moved south or to the Sahara before nature finished grinding down the North into nothing. After five winters like that, eighty years, there had not been much left.

"How much did you ever get to keep for your efforts, Shelton?" the priest said. "How much is going to the orphanage you name in your will?"

"About twenty thousand."

"From the sale of one—"

"Hey," I said. "We don't talk about that in here. This is a place of peace. Or it was until you guys showed up saying everything except what you really want."

"Then I'll be straight with you, Shelton Keyes: how would you like to unlock the door to the heavens?"

I pulled my arms and elbows behind me to lean back against the desk. This knocked my sketchbook onto the floor. The chaplain picked it up and set it on his lap.

"Wait," I said. "The lawyer said something about 'this world' not getting to me anymore. This experimental prison, are we talking about leaving Earth?"

The priest almost let himself smile. "Why didn't you make Officer Hernandez kill you?"

"Yes or no?"

The chaplain leafed through the pages of my sketchbook. "Which one of these women is the answer to my question?"

"None of them."

"To whom did you make your last phone call?"

That was to Mireille, to a number where she would receive messages. But I had not left a message; I had just choked out a breath and hung up. "No one."

"That makes my question more poignant, then. For what did you choose to live?"

"Money, I guess. I finally had some. Twenty grand. Money gives you something to live for."

"And those twenty thousand dollars you're leaving to an orphanage. But you're not an orphan."

"I had a good mother. I thought I'd give kids a chance who never did."

"A chance at what?"

"Life, you know."

"Yes, Shelton Keyes, life. Life is its own explanation. That's what this mission is about. Life. That's why you didn't pull your gun on Hernandez. No matter how hard you think you are, no matter how much you think you don't care, you're going to listen to life speaking inside you. That's why the IOSS and I have come to you."

Until he had said that, it had not occurred to me that I had been chosen for this project, that I had been to him anything more than the next guy onto the gurney.

"Well, you were almost too late," I said.

The priest stood up and said nothing to me but called in the warden and the lawyer. "He's ready."

The IOSS lawyer came in with the warden and laid out a folder on the desk. "Mr. Keyes, before you sign anything, I want to spell out some specifics for you. Project Abel is highly classified. You will become a privately held asset of the IOSS. You will, to the witnesses already gathering in the next room, appear to be executed by lethal injection. After that, you will be in our sole custody, with right over life and death. As for the money—"

"The orphanage," I said. "It's all spelled out in my will."

The lawyer looked confused. "How…anyway. The specifics of the project will be given to you at the assemblage site. I'm sorry, but I can say no more here."

"Where is the assemblage site?"

"I can say no more here."

"So that's it? I just sign, and then what?"

The priest pointed to the keys tattooed on my right hand and said, "Life."

The warden smiled. I signed, everyone left, and the fat guard locked the door.

The priest turned back. "The tattoo on your left hand, Shelton—it looks like a keyhole, but it's not, is it?"

It was the silhouette of a woman made to look like a keyhole. "It is not."

He fixed his eyes on me and said, "You're in good hands, Shelton Keyes."

I sat in the chair and looked at my cell in the death house. The bed was messed from where the priest had sat, and the whole place was humid and smelled of someone's cologne. Those were the only clues I had, in the re-ensuing silence, that any other life had been here at all, that I was not about to die.

2

"Shelton Keyes, it is time to come with me to the next room."

The warden said this, surrounded by the full tie-down team. An hour had passed. It was noon.

I closed my sketchbook and set the pencil on it.

"Your shoes, Keyes," the warden said.

I picked up the cheap canvas shoes. Before I died or went into space or whatever was about to happen, I wanted to feel the Earth again, or at least the cool floor of the death house.

The warden nodded and took the shoes from me.

Guards grabbed my arms and ushered me into the corridor. It was a twelve-foot walk to the door of the chamber.

It was bright inside, much brighter than my cell, and the room smelled like fresh vinyl. The gurney was black, almost in the shape of a body, arms sticking out from a square torso. It was a shadow version of me, my judgment in rectilinear shapes, a last glance at what my soul had become.

"You have two minutes for your last words," the warden said.

I looked at the two-way mirror, where I assumed Officer Ling's family had gathered and where no one on my side was sitting. All I saw was myself, the warden, and the tie-down team. The executioner was on the other side of a different wall.

"I'm sorry for what I done," I said. "For all I put you through."

After a few seconds, as if he was waiting for more, the warden said, "Sit down on the gurney and lie down on your back."

I did this. Four bright LED lights in the ceiling bleached out everything but the darkest dots in the acoustic tiles around them. Those black dots were my stars.

The guards tied down my arms, legs, and torso. All I heard was the warden saying something about the authority of the State of Florida. A nurse put an IV into my arm. Who knew what was really about to happen, whether I had dreamed up the conversation an hour ago or really was about to be sent to another prison. I looked at my toes and wiggled them. They were all I could see of my brown skin. I stretched to feel my body, the only thing that would tell me I was in a real place, and the priest urged me to keep calm.

He put his hand under my knee to feel my pulse and whispered a prayer, *"Deep calleth on deep, at the noise of thy flood-gates. All thy heights and thy billows have passed over me. In the daytime the Lord hath commanded his mercy; and a canticle to him in the night. With me is prayer to the God of my life."*

While I wondered what the connection was to my situation, I fell asleep.

3

When my eyes opened again, all I saw were my knees below me, still in my yellow jumpsuit. My butt hit hard against a metal seat, and my body shook sideways. I was in a metal cage, in a van with seven other inmates in cages wearing different-colored jumpsuits: orange, blue, and gray. My wrists were cuffed in front of me. My ankles were cuffed to a pole beneath the seat. The van smelled like vomit.

I rubbed my face. "Where are we?"

"Hell," someone said.

"Smells like it," I said and stretched my arms.

"Randall here gets carsick," someone else said.

I could not tell, through the layers of wire mesh, who had thrown up.

"This is a rough road," I said. "We've got to be up north somewhere."

"Seasick," the guy across from me said. "We are definitely on hover tech over water."

"That's a good way to crack the frame of a vehicle," another voice said.

"They've got to keep us low, out of sight," said the guy

across from me. "Remember, boys, this is all top secret. Hush hush."

There were no windows in the van. Light came from a single dim bulb in the ceiling.

"How long have we been driving?" I said.

"Since we picked you up, an hour perhaps," the guy across from me said. "I think we just hit the water when you woke up."

"Sal, I've got to pee," came a voice I had not yet heard, deep and halting, like a trombone in the hands of a toddler.

"Just go, Randall," Sal said. "Van already smells like puke thanks to you."

"I'm sorry," Randall said.

"Don't worry about it," Sal said. "Just take care of business. They'll get you a shower and fresh clothes when we get there."

"Where are we even at?" I said. "Hitting water after an hour from Raiford, that's either toward Houston or Atlantis."

"Houston means outer space," the guy across from me said. "My name is Cricket, by the way. Cricket St. Clair."

"Keyes," I said and turned away from his too-eager smile to find Randall. I still could not make out any more than the guy next to me, who had his eyes closed and was mouthing something. I looked down, between my feet, where a trickle of urine was following a groove in the floor. Someone at the death house at Florida State Prison had put my shoes back on.

"It's got to be Houston if we're really going off world," Cricket said. "They say Atlantis is all pottery shards and ancient spirits."

"I bet it's Atlantis we're going to," Sal said from the other end of the van. "That's where the IOSS and that witch who runs it hide all their darkest work."

"I heard they pulled you right off the gurney," Cricket said, apparently to me.

"You *saw*," said the man next to me, without opening his eyes. "You saw them carry him asleep into the van."

"Well, either way, right from the gurney to the van," Cricket said.

"They did that to all of us," Sal said. "Or at least to a holding cell, in my case. They want the world to think we're already dead. 'Death recorded,' as they say. An oxymoron if there ever was one."

"We're not all morons," said the guy next to me. "I'm a lifer. Simple as a transfer, and no one's the wiser."

He then vomited between his legs. A little splattered on me. I figured he had been keeping his eyes closed and his mouth moving with mantras to soothe his stomach. Driving low over water in hover tech was like riding a rollercoaster made of potholes.

"Damnit," Sal said. "Alright, guys, this is gonna get us all sooner or later. Ante up."

I had not eaten in at least three hours and had nothing to offer, but that did not keep the smell of vomit from inviting my stomach to do the same.

I closed my eyes and mouthed the last words I had heard the chaplain saying, *deep calls upon deep, deep calls upon deep*, until, a few minutes later, my stomach fell into my intestines.

"Hey, we're finally pulling up," Cricket said.

The rattling of wire mesh and the groans of puking prisoners gave way to a new sound, high-pitched, like a vacuum cleaner. It grew louder until the sound of the wind rushing past the van stopped. We were inside some other vehicle.

"We just air-docked inside a cargo plane," the guy next to me said. "Nice. Now, let us out." He banged the wall of the van. "Let us out."

For all I knew, we were already on a spaceship, but I was not going to argue with a guy who could project his puke onto me.

Muted voices came through the walls of the van, and thick snapping sounds came up through the floor. A couple of guys were laughing outside the rear doors right next to me.

"Any day now," the guy next to me said.

A buzzer went off, and the rear doors opened. Four guards in full turtle gear pointed guns at us.

The only thing louder than the guy next to me was the sound of six other inmates yelling to be let out so they could go to the bathroom and wash up. I looked past the guards to see the internal rib cage of a cargo plane lit in dull orange light.

"Count off," one of the guards said.

Cricket started at one, and the other guys followed. When the guy next to me said seven, I figured I was eight and said so.

"I wet myself," Randall said. He spoke with more proud assertion than simplicity.

"Number," the guard said.

"I went number one," Randall said, and again I could not tell if he was stupid or a smart-ass.

Sal coached him.

"Five," Randall said.

"One at a time," the guard said. "Open five."

"Opening five," another guard said.

The van rocked from side to side as Randall squeezed between the cages. He blocked the light when he passed me, and all I heard was flesh and fabric rubbing along the wire mesh. When he stepped off, the van lifted on its suspension.

"Damn, that's a big boy," one of the guards said.

"Grizzly bear," said another.

Their voices began to fade. "How do we get this puke off him?" "We've got water bottles." "Whole wagon smells like puke."

The guards stood ready, their guns pointed down.

"Hey, how much longer?" the guy next to me said.

"It's a few hours to assemblage," a guard said.

"How many?"

"A few."

"How fast are we flying?"

The guard did not answer.

"When do we eat? Some of us puked up our lunch."

It took half an hour for the guards to pull each inmate off the van separately so he could use the toilet. Being Number Eight, and having mostly clean clothes, I came out last.

There were seven other vans in the cargo hold of the plane. The rear doors were open to each of them; they were all full. That made sixty-four inmates on this project, so far.

The vans were each painted with the logo of Party Pig Catering, Inc.

"Number Three," someone said from a van I passed.

"You just went," a guard said.

"I've gotta go again."

The floor near the toilet was covered in dried vomit from where the guards had been washing it off prisoner jumpsuits. Our driver had not been the only one hovering low over the water, apparently.

When I came out of the bathroom, I saw a couple of guards standing around, drinking from water bottles. One of them pointed his bottle at me and said, "Hey. Good luck out there."

I looked at him, waiting for the punchline. He drank from his bottle, brought it down, and looked back at me. The guard taking me back to the van pulled on my arm.

"What was that all about?" I said, once we passed the first van.

"He was just wishing you good luck," the guard said. "Says that to everyone."

When I was locked in my cage again, I said to the guys, "The guards are kinda funny around here. You notice that?"

"They ain't prison guards," Number Two said. "These guys are paramilitary. Former special forces. The IOSS's own unit."

Not long after that, an IOSS guard handed out food—cold quesadillas, bananas, and drink boxes, basically the only things that would fit through the narrow slot in our cages. The guards were not unfriendly to us and let us out to use the bathroom again when we needed, but they gave us no information about where we were going or how long it would take to arrive.

4

We landed after six hours, according to Cricket's best estimate. From the Florida coast, that meant anywhere from San Francisco to the Azores, which everyone had dubbed Atlantis for the scattered traces of civilization the sinking seas had been uncovering for eighty years. The rear doors of the van closed again before the ramp of the cargo plane opened. We backed out on soft rubber tires, not hover tech, which could make the air feel like concrete, and drove for ten minutes before the rear doors opened again.

A gauntlet of helmets and guns met us. We were inside a warehouse, clean and brightly lit. The guards called us off the van one by one. I followed Cricket into a holding area arrayed with beds. There, I finally had a good look at him, Sal, Randall, and the other guys in my van. Cricket and Sal were white guys, probably both in their fifties, and Cricket had his hair pulled back with gel. Whereas Sal's eyes busily darted across the room, taking everything in, Cricket gazed with playacted serenity at each of us in turn. Randall was a side of beef, hide included, stuffed into an orange jumpsuit three sizes too small. His dark, glassy eyes lumbered menacingly from Sal to other things in the warehouse, as if measuring what was safe and what he had to kill.

Two guards followed us into the holding area; one carried a stack of zip-up portfolios in plasticky gray fabric.

"When I read your name, come forward and take your personal effects."

When Sal opened his, I saw letters in plastic sleeves and a thin photo album. Cricket did not open his. Mine had a few pictures I had left in my cell on death row stuffed into the plastic sleeves and, behind that, my sketchbook.

The inmates from the seven other vans slowly made their way into the holding area. While the guys were busy sizing each other up, I looked around.

The holding area, big enough to fit sixty-four beds and a platform, was a small part of the warehouse. Through the metal fencing, I could see a cafeteria, open showers, a few tanks for water or chemicals, very low and wide, and train tracks. There were, again, no windows, and the hangar doors were closed.

"Good evening, gentlemen," a guard said. He was standing on the platform between two other guards. "I am operations manager of this facility. Call me the warden of the warehouse, if you like. You are all still prisoners, in my custody. You will be here for less than one day. Until then, my job is to get your bodies, living or dead, into transport vessels. Your bodies are part of a very expensive investment the IOSS is making in conjunction with the Department of the Navy. If you incite violence or rioting, you will be shot on sight, and your dead body put into a transport vessel.

After that, it is up to God what happens to you. Understood? Good.

"Right now, we are putting you in new clothes. You will line up toward the showers. You will put the clothes you are currently wearing into the gray barrels at the entrance to the showers. After you shower, you will put on a new jumpsuit. After that, you will proceed through the door at the other end of the showers, into the mess hall, for dinner. Any questions? Good. Line up."

A few guys shouted out questions about where we were, the details of Project Abel, making phone calls and emails, and what was coming tomorrow. To each of these questions, the warehouse warden answered with the same three words spit out in the same order: *Shower. Clothes. Dinner.*

Sal encouraged Randall to push his way to the head of the line, and between the man's sheer size and the lingering smell of puke and piss on his clothes, no one was going to argue. Since the other occupants of our van had been standing around Randall, this meant we went first, too.

One guard took the cuffs off my wrists and tossed them into a gray plastic barrel. Another guard did the same for my ankles. I slipped out of my shoes and discovered that the concrete floor was warm. I tossed the shoes into another gray plastic barrel and stepped forward to take off my yellow jumpsuit and underwear. My skin grew hot and glowed slightly red—there was an electric heater above the door to the showers.

There was a fresh bar of soap in the stall, meaning I did not have to rinse someone else's hair off it first. The water was hot. There was no towel waiting for me, only white briefs, a zip-up orange jumpsuit made of thick, high-tech fabric, and black rubber sandals. Combs were available in jars full of disinfecting solution.

My mouth was watering before I even saw what was in the kitchen. There was a buffet line, and the first things I noticed were piles of fried chicken. I picked up a plastic tray and heavy-duty plastic plate and loaded up on fried chicken, mashed potatoes, carrots, and broccoli.

"Do you see this?" I said to Sal, next to me in line.

The guard serving us looked at my plate and said, "Don't worry. You can always come back for seconds. There's plenty."

To whoever was listening, I said, "It's like they're half treating us like animals and half like kings."

At the end of the line was a table with paper napkins—and metal forks and knives. Sal picked up a fork and knife. He studied them quickly, eyed the guard, looked at me, and turned to study the room filling with inmates.

"Metalware? I don't think this is a good idea," I said and took a fork and knife.

Sal shook his head.

Sal, Randall, and I sat at one of the circular tables. A tall, lanky guy not from our van walked up to the table and nodded to Sal, who stuck out his chin toward the empty seat.

The man took his seat and said, "Holsworthy. Launce Holsworthy."

"Where from?" Sal said.

"Leavenworth," Launce said. "Before that, the Blue Ridge Mountains."

There was a big gap from the Blue Ridge Mountains to

military prison, but I would let Sal work the conversation. My first time in jail—even entering a police station, for that matter—was for killing a cop. After a quick trial, I had been sent directly to death row. The justice system worked pretty smoothly these days. I counted on that to survive. After ten months on death row, I knew almost nothing about etiquette in general population.

"Sal Combes," Sal said and nodded toward Randall.

"I'm Randall Chudleigh."

"Shelton Keyes," I said. "Florida State."

No one said much after that.

"Look at this knife," came a voice from behind me. "I could stab you with this knife."

Sal was staring behind me.

"Don't mess around, man," another voice said.

When that conversation quieted down, Launce said, "That was some ride out here."

"Yeah," Sal said. His eyes were darting across the room. "I hope it's smoother sailing after this."

"Yeah," Launce said.

Randall, with grease covering his mouth and fingers, said, "Sal, can I get some more?"

"Why are you asking me? You heard the guard yourself. Load up. Just don't make yourself puke it all up again."

"How long have you known Randall?" I said.

Sal's eyes widened, and he dropped his drumstick. He reached out to me. Before I could finish wondering what was wrong with what I had said, I heard behind me shouting, a brief noise like a whistle, and heavy boots. A body dropped right next to my feet. It smelled of burnt clothes and looked like grilled chicken. Four guards carried it away.

Guys stood around the space the dead inmate left behind.

Launce turned from his plate and said, "That's what a charged devonium spear point will do to you."

The warden stood on a box in the cafeteria and said, "That's one dead body we're shipping into space. Make a choice, gentlemen. Live like kings, eating your dinner with fork and knife, or die like that. When you are in space, you will have many tools at your disposal, many of them deadly. They are there to help you in your work against the forces of nature. But whereas natural forces kill gradually, special forces kill quickly. Make your choice." He stepped down again.

One of the guys at the next table said, "He just made to stab me. I just met the guy. Why would he stab me?"

"Because he had a knife," Launce said, quietly amongst ourselves, and bit into his fried chicken.

"Better safe than sorry," Sal said. "Let's watch each other's backs here."

I did not want anyone to see that my hands were shaking, so I picked up a piece of chicken with both hands and propped my elbows on the table. That had been one of the few points of etiquette my mother had ever insisted on, maybe one of the few she had known. *Sorry, Mom.* I chewed my food slowly so my tightening throat would not choke on it.

"Like I was saying," Launce said. "These guys are sharpshooters, every single one of them. Special forces. These are the kind of guys who were standing on the wall after the moondark when demons started creeping out of the sea."

Launce was referring to what had happened eighty years ago.

I, like many, did not believe that spirits or specters of any kind had come out of the sea after the moon turned off like a lightbulb and a new ice age started on Earth. How those two events were related, I did not know, though they taught it in school. All I did know was that when ice started covering the most northern and southern parts of Earth, it sucked up water from the ocean. People had the craziest theories about the age in which we had been living, including that Earth had turned inside out and wrapped around the moon, and that the moon had become a portal to the rest of the universe. People would believe anything to make reality more bearable. For me, reality was simple: everyone had to move south. Life was topsy-turvy, and that had made people see ghosts. Once everyone had settled down again, the specters had stopped coming. Quite a coincidence.

I heard Randall laughing behind me. He had a bowl of ice cream in his hand and was praising a guard for the kill shot he had just taken, trying to make the soldier, still holding his rifle, give Randall a high-five.

The guards did not push us out of the mess hall and let us linger there for a while. Guys started leaving in groups, more or less the way I knew they hung out in general population: Blacks with Blacks, Asians with Asians, white guys with swastikas, white guys without swastikas, Hispanics with tattoos, Hispanics with different tattoos. Sal pointed his chin at me. I did not know if he was inviting me to leave with the Black guys or what. None of those groups were mine, not before prison or inside it.

"Where are you from?" Sal said.

"St. Louis," I said.

"What neighborhood?"

"My mom's white, if that's what you're asking."

"And your dad?" Launce said, joining in.

"Beats me."

Sal leaned back, took a deep breath, and patted his belly. "Good meal. Keep your knives."

We stood up to leave. A metal detector went off at the door leading out of the cafeteria. The guys ahead of us, who had also thought to keep their knives, had to give them up. In fact, the warden had already wheeled over to the door a plastic tray, into which we all threw our utensils.

Once inside the holding area, Sal starting making the rounds, figuring out who was who. I found a cot in the corner. Cricket took the cot next to mine, trying to make it look like it was the last one available. Randall walked straight toward him and told him that was his cot. Cricket was not going to argue. I looked toward Sal, in the middle of the holding area, and caught him turning his head away. He had sent Randall. I did not know who Sal was, but he took care of his own. So far, I fit in here.

5

I woke up, the next morning, to the lights above the holding area of the warehouse going on all at once. For those who slept through that, a buzzer tore at our ears. I had slept soundly, though. After the sharpshooting demonstration at dinner, I had not been worried about being knifed in my sleep.

When I put my feet on the floor, I noticed that everyone had plastic boxes at the foot of their cots. I had one, too. They had not been there last night. This was another demonstration that the guards had total control, that they could move sixty-three plastic trunks in complete silence.

"I noticed them," Cricket said. He had found another cot nearby. "Some of us are light sleepers. Others of us are snorers."

I opened my trunk, which had my name on it. Inside were boots, several pairs of socks and thermal underwear, a second, heavier jumpsuit, and a vacuum-sealed bag labeled *Winter Gear*.

"Good morning, gentlemen," the warden said from the platform. "I hope you are well rested. You have a long day ahead of you. Next to your cots, as many of you have already noticed, is a trunk. Inside that trunk are footwear, toiletries, and winter clothes. Do not open the bag of winter clothes, or you will find yourself very cramped and wanting for space inside your vehicle. Those bags are vacuum-sealed for your convenience. Like the boots and underclothes inside, they are measured to your size."

The boots were regular work boots, size nine. They were not the kind of boots I imagined astronauts wore.

"Put on your socks and boots, then line up for breakfast."

I could already smell sizzling bacon.

"Are we eating the guy you fried last night?" someone called out.

A few guys laughed.

"Socks, boots, breakfast," the warden said.

"Socks, boots, breakfast," a few guys repeated, and before long, all sixty-three of us were chanting in unison: *Socks. Boots. Breakfast.*

"That's the spirit," the warden said. "We'll make a corps out of you, yet."

***

After a breakfast of eggs, bacon, and hash browns, and before I could finish studying the contents of my trunk, the buzzer sounded, and the warden ordered us to stand. A door opened at a far corner of the warehouse, and a string of silhouetted bodies darkened the rectangle of white light the open door had made. When they came closer, my eyes fixed on one woman, small in stature, who walked with the same kind of unpracticed severity that the priest with the cane had yesterday, in the death house. When the suits and uniforms lined up on a platform outside the fence to the holding area, she stood in the middle.

The warden ordered us to make sure our boots were tied, to put our portfolio of personal effects into our trunks, to pick up our trunks, and to proceed with them, in an orderly fashion, to the assembly area on the other side of the fence. We would not be returning to our cots. Not ever.

We lined up in the assembly area, with our trunks on the floor in front of us, in eight rows of eight inmates, minus one.

"Gentlemen," the warden said. "Before your eyes are the leaders of Project Abel. They represent the brightest minds at the International Office of Special Science and the Department of the Navy. You will give them your full and undivided attention. As for these gentlemen, ma'am…."

The small woman was certainly in charge. This was the head of the IOSS. I did not know her name.

"…they are the best behaved group of trusties I have so far encountered. We are sixty-four bodies total, as ordered. Sixty-three living, one dead."

"Thank you, warden," the woman said. She nodded to a smiling man in a suit next to her.

The man stepped forward and said, "Welcome to Project Abel. This is a joint effort by the IOSS and US Navy to build lines of communication with potentially habitable worlds. You, men, are at the vanguard of a new age of human discovery."

The warden had used the word "trusty." I had learned about prisons where they had that system, where guys were earning time off through hard labor. We were probably being sent to break rocks for someone else to build on. But there was no time off a death sentence.

"My name is Dr. Lewis Trenchard, deputy director of the IOSS," the man said. "You all know, I'm sure, Dr. Doris Huntsman, our esteemed director."

That was the small woman standing at the center.

Dr. Trenchard continued, "The moon, as you know, was first made through the physical collision of another planet with Earth, at the very beginnings of our solar system. At the Merge, eighty years ago, the Earth reclaimed the moon, but not in a purely physical way. The moon went dark, transformed into a sphere of dark matter incapable of reflecting or emitting electromagnetic radiation, what we call the moonshock. At the same time, the Earth began taking on the moon's qualities, including an eighteen-year precession of the polar axis. This has meant, as you all know, a crushing arctic winter circling Earth's upper latitudes every eighteen years, pushing what has remained of humanity into the former tropics. The moon's inability to reflect light and radio waves, as well, began to frustrate all radio communications on Earth, as it has to this day."

We had all learned this in school.

"You have all learned this in school, I'm sure. What you have not learned is that, just over fifty years ago, the US Navy and the IOSS, known then as the OSS, first breached the moonshock. That's right, gentlemen. We have already breached the portal and gone to other planets."

The man paused, as if waiting for gasps of wonder from the inmates. All the guys did, though, was murmur about how they had known that all along, that what for fifty years had been going around as conspiracy theory was now proven fact. They would, of course, admit it only to people who were about to die.

"Today, gentlemen, is going to be a day of equal importance. For fifty years, the IOSS has been developing ways of repeating the experience of breeching the moonshock. We have succeeded. And you are the ones going through this time, to build a bridge for us to follow."

I looked from side to side at the guys around me. Some were smirking, others were misty-eyed. I did not know what I felt. Then, someone else shouted it out.

"I get it, you're throwing your garbage out into space to see what sticks."

A lot of the guys laughed at this. No one on stage so much as blinked.

A minute passed, while the other inmates still cracked jokes, until some kind of pulse hit us from the rafters of the warehouse. It was a slow, suffocating sonic pulse. Everyone stopped talking. The pulsing stopped.

The warden stepped forward. "You want respect, gentlemen, and you've got it, so long as you give it in return. Understand what these fine people are saying to you. Once you leave here, you're free to live or die on your terms, in whatever way these other planets make possible."

"Give us a few more minutes of your attention," Trenchard said, "and the rest of your lives are your own."

One inmate raised his hand. Trenchard put his palm up to ask him to wait, but Dr. Huntsman pulled his arm down and pointed and nodded to the inmate.

"Are we gonna face the specters out there, like our grandparents did here?"

Trenchard said, "The chances of encountering intelligent life of any kind are negligible."

"That includes us," someone yelled out.

While the guys laughed at this, another inmate raised his hand. "Where are the women?" he said.

The guys hooted and whistled.

"No, I'm serious now," the inmate said. "You want us to go and build a civilization on an alien planet with no women? That might work for some of these wolves here but not for me."

Huntsman glanced next to her at a much taller woman in military uniform, who stepped forward.

"Now we're talking," I said, apparently not quietly enough, because the sonic pulse came back down, and on my head only, from what I could tell. I looked around and patted my chest, to admit my fault. The suffocating pulse stopped.

"Gentlemen," the military woman said, "I am Lieutenant Commander Sabina Baron-Gold, chief operations officer. We are, in fact, sending a group of female inmates, a much smaller group. They will launch with you. But you will not end up at the same location. There is no purpose in that. I want to say to you bluntly that the environments to which you are being sent will not, for some time, be conducive to civilization, to supporting a family."

"Say that again?" the same inmate said.

"It is most likely that you will be the first living things on these planets," Baron-Gold said.

No one said anything for a few seconds until another hand came up.

"That's it," the guy said. "My name is Bel Chichacott, and I've heard enough. This project is in violation of a number of human-rights laws. Shall I list them for you? First of all, cruel and unusual punishment. Sending us to slowly starve to death in a hostile environment is no way to treat another human being even if he's on death row. Secondly, what kind of cooperation do you expect from men with clearly defective affect and manifest criminal proclivities? Once we get there, we'll all just kill each other, just like we started to do last night. But maybe that's what you want, to send us up as fertilizer for the next batch of colonizers to grow their gardens. Even at our best, are we really the ones you want representing humanity to other planets? And we are untrained as astronauts. Why not send soldiers? Why are you not sending your own soldiers into space?"

The men applauded, myself included.

Dr. Huntsman let a smile slip across her face, and her eyes brightened like stars in a black sky. She was, I realized, a beautiful woman. In this situation, maybe that meant nothing; maybe she really was a witch, as Sal had said yesterday, but Bel's opening her up this way, making this woman beautiful to me, made me respect the man who had just spoken. If I could choose, I would ride up to space with Bel. He seemed intelligent, anyway, and sure of himself.

Dr. Huntsman stepped forward. Maybe it was the witchcraft in her step, or maybe just total confidence, but all the guys quieted down quickly.

"Would you all kindly take a seat?" she said. "Your trunks are sturdy enough to sit on."

Like kindergarteners at story time, sixty-three grown men sat down to listen.

"It's not as simple, Mr. Chichacott, as sending you up to serve as fertilizer. Men, every single one of you agreed to partake in this mission based on limited information. For that, we thank you. You are, for the most part, death-row inmates who have lost all your appeals, and your sentence has not been commuted. Some of you are serving one or more life sentences, and you have agreed to spend the rest of your life sentence in this experimental prison colony.

"None of you, in the eyes of earthly justice, or in the hearts of your fellow human beings, deserves another minute of life. And that makes you the ideal candidates. You are murderers, thieves, and rapists—and you are the best hope for humanity. Your past is dark, but the future belongs to those who do new things. Your mere presence in these other worlds will send a clear signal back to us, a signal we can follow with the rest of humanity. That line of communication is our best hope, and yours."

"What other worlds?" Bel said. "Where exactly are we going?"

Huntsman breathed in deeply and said, "The word 'exactly' is not applicable from our present position."

"English, doc," someone called out.

"We have access to other worlds, but we do not know where they are. Once you are there, we will know where they are."

Bel said, "How are you going to point the rocket if you don't know where we're going?"

"That's proprietary knowledge."

Some of the guys groaned and sighed.

Huntsman caught Bel's eyes and said, "Mr. Chichacott, we have sent soldiers. Many brave soldiers. We know the technology works. But a telephone wire is only as good as the conversation it carries. That's why we want you. To send a clear signal."

Dr. Doris Huntsman, director of the IOSS, held her gaze on Bel. I watched her bewitch him. If the guys said anything after that, I did not hear it.

Lights went on in the back of the warehouse. Behind Huntsman and the other speakers were the wide, low drums I had seen yesterday. What I had not noticed, in the shadows, were the small gasket windows on them.

"Gentlemen," Lieutenant Commander Baring-Gold said, "these are your vehicles."

One of vehicles came forward on the sunken train tracks and stopped in front of her, at her feet. It looked about ten feet tall and twice as wide, made of smooth gray metal, with only a few markings on the outside.

"It looks like a can of tuna," Sal said.

Baring-Gold stood aside while, from behind her on the stage, a wedged-shaped box was brought out, closed on all sides except the one facing us. From where I sat, all I could see was a black chair turned sideways.

"Is that the cockpit?" Launce said after raising his hand.

"It is a model of your cell. In each module, each tuna can, as you call it, there are nine cells of this size and shape.

Eight are identical to this. The ninth is a vestibule, having the only door that opens horizontally. The eight other cells are accessible only from hatches in the ceiling."

She opened the ceiling hatch on the model cell.

"This circulation pattern is to prevent movement between cells during flight. It ensures security. After what happened last night, I'm sure each of you would appreciate the precautions. No one person will be able to threaten the lives of others. Even if your tear your own cell apart, you will not be damaging the module."

I resisted looking at the other guys to see if any of them were as glad as I was to be kept safe from psychopaths. I was sure I had not been the only one scared last night, but I would not be the first to admit it.

Baring-Gold continued, "Each cell is fully functional. You have your own touchscreen monitor from which you have access to all computer functions, including flight controls. Each of you can steer the whole module from your seat. You can take turns flying without leaving your cells."

"Flying?" someone said.

A young officer sat down in the model cell, tapped a few times on the screen in front of him, and began rubbing his finger along it. The tuna can on the train tracks below began moving forward, by remote control. He used a second finger, and the whole module started lifting off the ground. He raised it higher than Baring-Gold's head, where we could all see it was on hover tech.

"We get our own damn flying saucer," someone said.

I said, "Ha! We're the aliens now."

Huntsman caught my eye, all the way in the back corner.

She must have seen the dumb smile on my face. For all her talk about our being the best hope for humanity, the thing that made me want to do this now was to fly my own spaceship.

"She should have just led with this," Cricket said.

I had not noticed he was nearby.

"I mean, my God."

6

It was a couple more hours of tutorials by officers and technicians. We saw the parts of the module: drawers that opened from outside filled with gardening tools, survival gear, inflatable boats, and small tents; a large tent tucked into the upper ring, which, when pulled across the top of the module, made a dome shape. The cells inside had their own storage, too, and individual floor toilets, Turkish-style, that emptied into trays of cat litter below our cells. Our food would be something they called High-Density Rations, thick wafers of green, fibrous stuff we would have to rehydrate before eating. We had a year's supply, each, along with powdered juice, coffee, and tea. We had a year to plant and harvest our own food with seed packets they supplied, or a year to hope that other humans would follow us to the planet with more food.

During a break, a few guys approached the warden, who in turn brought Dr. Huntsman over to the conversation. They looked like the same guys who had held a prayer service for the inmate killed at dinner.

Everyone else kept to the groups they had formed at dinner. The IOSS had said nothing about module assignments. I searched out Sal, figuring he would put together a good team, but I could not keep his attention. Cricket stood back, watching me. Before I could talk to Bel, the warden announced it was time to start loading.

The guys who had been talking to Huntsman and the warehouse warden lined up outside the module already on the train tracks, the one used in our demonstration. This module was marked with a large two—eight women were already loaded into Module One, the IOSS said, somewhere we could not see them. I watched as the body of the dead inmate, in a body bag, was lowered through the upper hatch of one of the cells in the module. A specialist had already gone in to receive the body and buckle it in. Seven other inmates then handed their trunks to a guard on top of the module, walked through the door of the vestibule, climbed the ladder inside the vestibule to the roof of the module, and lowered themselves through the hatches of the individual cells. I saw their faces through the gasket windows.

One specialist confirmed that they were all strapped in, and another knocked on the wall of the can. It started hovering along the tracks toward the far wall of the warehouse, where it stopped. Two guards stood on top of the module, back to back, as it hovered. The hatches were still open.

I looked again for Sal but could not find him.

Bel was in a far back corner, arms crossed, stroking a soft chin covered in five-o'clock shadow. He was about my height but older, perhaps older than Sal and Cricket, a little pudgy, and mostly bald on top. He looked like he had spent most of his time reading.

"We who are about to die salute you!"

The self-appointed leader of a second group held his arm out straight in salute to Huntsman and her team.

"Come on, gladiators," he said. "Let's go kick some alien ass."

He slapped the side of Module Three as he passed through the vestibule, and the seven who followed him did the same. Before descending into their individual cells, they stood in a circle on top of their can and saluted the rest of us in unison.

"God bless America," the leader said and climbed down into his cell.

Four more modules filled up the same way, with diminishing enthusiasm among those who boarded them. I still could not find Sal or Randall, and Bel was sulking in the corner. Cricket had not budged. Launce, too, was hanging around.

Right before Module Eight came down the tracks, Sal returned to the assembly area with Randall.

"You coming or what?" Sal said to me.

"What about Bel?" I said.

"What about him? I've got a group together here."

I tapped the side of my head. "Don't we need some brains with us?"

"Sal," Launce said from behind me.

Sal looked at him then to where Bel was standing. Sal knit his brow then shrugged. He turned to the guys lined up for Module Eight and motioned for one of them to come over.

"Maybe you're right, Sal," he said. He was a tall, muscular Black guy with a shaved head. "The last shall be first."

The guards looked at the warden, who looked to Huntsman for instruction. She whispered to the warden, who pointed to three of the guys still waiting around. Guards pulled them into the line for Module Eight to replace Sal, Randall, and the Black guy. Module Eight filled and hovered down the tracks, where it waited in line with the other six.

Module Nine hovered toward us. My stomach twisted. It looked identical to all the other cans, but this one was mine. I would be in that module, and I would not see the outside of it again until I was on an alien planet. I looked around the warehouse for one last glimpse of Earth. When I lowered my head again, I saw my team: Sal, Randall, Cricket, Launce, and Bel; the tall, muscular Black guy with a shaved head who had said "the last shall be first"; and a skinny guy whose face, neck, and arms were covered in tattoos, likely a Central American gang member. We were the last of the inmates.

Doris Huntsman was standing by the door to the vestibule this time. She had not come down to see off any of the other modules.

"Now or never," I said.

Bel, with his foot locker in hand, pushed through our group and was the first to the vestibule door.

I could not read Huntsman's lips to hear what she said to him, but he ignored her and climbed up the vestibule ladder to the roof of the module, where a specialist told him which cell to take.

The four biggest guys were brought through next so they could be assigned cells for weight distribution. We all stood in wonder as Randall squeezed through the vestibule door and then through the smaller upper hatch of the vestibule. Even Huntsman raised her eyebrows.

"I'm an octopus," he said.

The rest of us looked at each other, wondering what he meant.

I heard a brief shout and looked back. Two guards and a specialist were holding Randall's arms. He had lost his balance and had almost fallen off the module.

"Some octopus," Sal said.

"How long have you known him?" I asked again.

"Me?" Sal said. "I just met him yesterday, in the van."

"But you're already acting like his caretaker."

"I guess it comes natural." Sal then entered the module.

I was last in line, somehow. I handed my trunk to the guard above.

"Let me see those hands," Huntsman said to me.

I held up my tattoos for her to see. She held my fists in her hands. I felt electricity flowing over me like a gentle creek. This was not witchcraft, just womanhood. I had felt this touch before.

A guard reached out, but she cast him a quick glance, and he backed down.

"I understand the crossed keys, Mr. Keyes. But tell me about the lock you have on your left hand, shaped like a woman. What does she represent?"

"Reality, ma'am."

"That's not a common place for men to keep women."

"I'm an uncommon man, Dr. Huntsman."

"We'll see about that," she said and let go of my hands.

"Reality is about to become a lot different for you. For all of you. Hold onto what is real, for everyone's sake."

I looked at the window of the cell closest to me to see who was watching this exchange. The window was empty. That was my cell, right next to the vestibule.

I rubbed the side of the can and slapped it. The vestibule, all white inside, had a few drawers in it, a fire extinguisher, and a defibrillator behind glass. I climbed the ladder inside to the roof. From the top of the module, I had a view of the whole warehouse—the cots, the kitchen, and the bathroom—and of the seven modules lined up in front of us. My cell was small, with just enough room to stand next to the seat and not enough to stretch out my arms. I sat down and buckled in. Huntsman was not outside the window anymore.

On the floor, at the base of the ladder into the cell where the squat toilet was hidden under a cover panel, I saw a black-and-yellow strip and the words *Radiation Warning*.

"Naturally, with the nuclear-waste-colored rations we're gonna eat," I said out loud.

"Who are you talking to?" came a voice from the computer screen in front of me.

"What?"

"We can all talk to each other through the computer." A tag appeared on screen, *Cell Six*. It sounded like Bel.

All secured, came a voice from above.

The module started hovering forward.

"I think it's time we all got to know each other," came another voice, from Cell Two, next to mine. His face came on video. It was the only other Black guy in Module Nine, the last-shall-be-first. "I'll begin. My name is Prosper. No, that is not the name my mother gave me. But that is how I would like to be known. We are a new family. No need for other names. Or, if you choose to give me a family name, make it Us."

"Prosperous?" I said.

"No, Prosper Us, as in, may God prosper us on this mission to find new worlds in His name."

"Amen," Bel said. "But we're going to have a lot of time for chitchat later on. We've got a thirty-minute trip to the launch site, and I would like to know as much as I can about this system before we get thrown into space."

Through the window, I could see the far wall of the warehouse suddenly awash in bright light.

"They opened the hangar doors," Bel said.

We started moving over the train tracks, not under our own control. Soon, daylight poured down through the open hatch to my cell. I could smell the sea. Once outside the warehouse, I saw blue sky, bare rock, and metal fencing in between. A few jeeps were parked nearby. A specialist motioned us forward. The module was slowly rotating.

A voice came through the speaker: *Now that you're moving, let me explain a few more things.* It was Dr. Trenchard. *First, the rotation you're experiencing is normal. It is the effect of the superconducting coils in your main hover engine spinning over the magnetic chain you're riding out to the launch site. When you are hovering on your own, you will not experience this rotation.*

The can in front of us came into view. I nodded to the guy in the window.

You will gain control of the module once you've penetrated new air space. Your seat buckles will unlock once you've completed the launch procedure, in two hours' time.

I tried my buckle. It would not unclasp. "Man, I hope Randall went before we left."

Sal's voice came on. "It was for this precise reason that I took him to the bathroom before we boarded."

In the meantime, learn the system.

"One step ahead of you," Bel said.

Very importantly, when you do use the toilet, do not linger there. You see a line on the floor marked Radiation Warning. *At the center of each module is a small nuclear reactor.*

"The hell there is," Launce said.

The reactor does not power the engines directly. It charges the batteries underneath the module. It would take a much larger reactor to power your engines. You will have limited flight time between hops, depending on altitude, speed, wind, and weight.

Like everything about prison, power was enforced through time.

Do not eat any of your rations until after launch. We carefully timed launch to well over three hours past breakfast. We don't want anyone to vomit.

"Oops," Randall said, and I could hear the crinkling of a paper wrapper through the computer speaker.

While Trenchard continued to talk, I scrolled through the menus on the computer, trying to learn the system, too.

The module jolted. I looked outside. It was open ocean, all the way to the horizon. We were, once again, on hover tech over water. As the module rotated, I could see the land we had left, with the warehouse in the distance. The train tracks continued over the water. Waves lapped over them.

"How are these tracks held up?" I said out loud.

Some of you are wondering about the floating chain you're following. This is the result of eleven kilowatts of electricity being pumped into devonium alloy, also known as orichalcum. Welcome to Atlantis, gentlemen.

PART TWO

SEPARATE

7

Thirty-three minutes after leaving the warehouse, we reached the launch site. The warehouse and the bare rocky island on which it sat had long ago fallen past the horizon. The only things interrupting my view of the open ocean had been Module Eight in front of us, a few Navy boats following us, and, looming larger with each rotation of the can, a metal gantry. We hovered a few feet above the tracks, just higher than the mid-Atlantic waves. No one in my module said much while we each studied the system through videos on the computer.

They had shown us a rocket in our orientation video a couple of hours ago, and the computer screen in front of me showed the status of a rocket: a large central tube with smaller rocket tubes attached to the side. I could not see it through the window of my cell.

A metal gangway started running parallel to the track. *Closing One*, came the voice of one of the guards on top of our module. *Closing Two*. At *Closing Nine*, my ceiling hatch closed, the cell went dark, a small light came on, and air conditioning started blowing from a vent beneath my seat. I could hear the two guards descending the ladder in the vestibule next to me. *Closing vestibule hatch*, came a voice through the computer. *Closing module door*, came a muffled sound from outside. After the thud it made, I could hear only the air conditioning and my heart beat. Through the window, I saw the two guards walking down the metal gangway.

Module One ready, came another voice through the computer. This was the women's module. A diagram showed it attached to the pulley.

"Why don't they just hover it in?" said Sal from Cell Three.

Even I knew the answer to that question. "Because they'd burn up whatever's below them."

"Right," Sal said.

The diagram showed the pulley lowering Module One into the large tube of the rocket. Then I understood: the rocket was in the water. We were going to launch out of the water.

No one was wondering about this, so I said, "Do y'all know why we're launching from the water, not Houston? Did they explain this?"

"What do any of us know about rocket science?" Sal said.

"We're gonna be astronauts in a few minutes. They should tell us something about it."

A brief chuckle came through the intercom. *Who said you were astronauts?* It was Trenchard.

"Aren't we going into space?"

No one said that.

"How else are we getting to other planets?"

Trenchard did not answer.

When the pulley fitted Module Eight into the rocket, my window was facing the sea behind us. The launch site was behind me, and so I could not see it. After hearing all the official chatter for loading Module Eight, I felt the magnetic hooks cling to the upper ring of my module, Module Nine. We lifted off the track a few feet. Specialists in hard hats stood on the circular gangway surrounding the open mouth of the rocket. We swung a little, and I could briefly see the upper edge of the open tube below. Waves splashed into the rocket tube, and this did not seem to bother anyone. We stopped swinging. *We have alignment.* Module Nine lowered, and the rim of the rocket rose past my window. Dim orange light crept into my cell.

A woman with a computer tablet stood outside my window. The rocket tube was really a launch tube, filled with walkways and stairs. I was no rocket scientist, but this seemed like an awful waste of space. Something clicked below my feet. *Module Nine engaged.*

"Here we go, boys," Cricket said.

No one answered.

The diagram on the computer showed what looked like a nose cone being lifted on top of us. This part of the rocket made sense to me. It clicked to our can, above my head.

Pilot module secured, a technician said.

Ladies and gentlemen, Trenchard said, *meet your pilots, Lieutenants Ash and Willand. They will be your ferry boat captains, taking you down to the floor.*

"Down?" I said.

Clear the launch tube, a technician said. The woman

outside my window walked away. I heard a lot of muted footsteps on metal grating.

Ladies and gentlemen, you are about to be launched into the abyss. It was Trenchard again. *To accomplish this, we are lowering you to the ocean floor. Because we cannot communicate with you effectively with radio, we have to physically push you down. That is the role of the pilot module. As for you, do not worry about oceanic pressure or g-forces from launch. They will not be a factor. It will be a slow descent, lasting approximately one hour, until you reach a depth of eighty-four hundred feet. We will communicate again when you reach depth.*

Flood the ballast tubes.

On the display, the four tubes I had taken for external rocket engines each showed a percentage while they filled with water. Nothing else on the diagram looked like an engine except the four squares below them marked *Weights*.

The rocket, which seemed to be nothing more than a stack of tuna cans with a pilot module on top, gently swayed with the launch tube as it sank, like I was sitting on the top branch of a tree in the wind.

"My brothers," Prosper said, "we still have an hour while we sink to the launch site, whatever that means. May I humbly suggest we get to know each other a little now? Learning the system is good, but learning each other is better. We've got to rely on each other now. The hatches are closed, and they aren't going to open again until the light of new sun shines on our faces. Can I suggest we start with Cell One? Brother, would you kindly introduce yourself?"

That was me. "Alright, uh, Shelton Keyes, from STL the

new DC. Twenty-one years old. Murder One, of a police officer in the line of duty."

Someone whistled. I had learned before that not every criminal was in favor of killing cops. But I was not a career criminal, like these guys. I had to step forward so they would think I was on equal terms. And so they knew I was not a chomo.

"How'd you end up in Florida from Saint Louis?" Prosper said.

"Business. I am a collector."

"Debt collector?" Prosper said.

"He means scavenger," Cricket said.

"I'll tell you what I mean," I said. "I am a collector of art and antiques. I save a world from getting lost under the long winter."

"That is a noble line of work," Prosper said. "Keeping the old world alive. Do you want to add anything, Keyes?"

"No, I'm alright."

"Fine, then. Moving on to cell number two, once again, my name is Prosper. I am forty-three years old, from Huntsville, Alabama. I am a lifer, justly condemned for my crimes. But you can read my papers on the computer. I do not wish to give voice to them. For me, this is a fresh start. I am a new man. And you, my brothers, are my family. As the apostle Paul says, *We are made as the filth of the world, and are the offscouring of all things, appointed to death, made a spectacle unto the world, and to angels, and to men*. The men of this world *have reigned as kings without us*, but I say we will be the kings of our own land, eight kings of one kingdom. That is how I see it, brothers, and Dr. Huntsman, if you are listening. Though *we both hunger and thirst, and are naked, and are buffeted, and have no certain dwelling place, and labor, working with our own hands,* God will bless all that we do, and bring our brothers and sisters to us, and no one can claim we were worthless in the end."

"Preach it, brother," Sal said. "My name is Sal Combes, Cell Three, forty-eight years old. I appreciate your point of view, Prosper. But some of us are leaving a lot behind. We're not doing this for strictly noble reasons."

"You talking about the money?" Prosper said.

"I am precisely talking about the money," Sal said. "I've got a wife and two teenaged kids back home. This was the only way I was going to help them."

I tried to sit forward, but the seat belt held me back. "What money would that be?"

"The thirty grand," Sal said.

"What thirty grand?" I said.

Prosper said, "Were you not offered the king's ransom? Perhaps they gave you less, being a young man, and single."

"Did y'all get that much?" I said. "And who said I was single?"

The other guys confirmed they had.

"I mean, yeah," I said. "Of course I got it. And don't tell me I've got nothing left behind. I've got plenty of people relying on me back home. Including a girl. Mireille's her name."

By that, I meant an orphanage full of children and Mireille, whom I would never see again except in my sketchbook. But no one had offered me thirty thousand dollars.

"Alright," Prosper said. "Let's keep going. How about our brother in Cell Four?"

"My name is Cricket St. Clair. And, yes, that is the name my momma gave me. I'm from Charlotte, North Carolina. Read my papers all you want, but let me emphasize that I did not commit the heinous crime for which I was so unjustly convicted."

"Then why did you agree to this project?" Prosper said.

"It sounded better than rotting away on death row. A chance to do something positive."

"Amen, brother," Prosper said. "How about Cell Five, now?"

"Uh, yeah, so, Launce here, Cell Five. Launce Holsworthy. Former Navy sub scout. Sent to Leavenworth. It was an honest mistake."

"You're the ringer," Sal said. "You can pilot this thing."

"I sure can," Launce said. "But I'll teach y'all how to drive it, too."

I looked around my cell and said, "What's this thing we're in, anyway? It's like a sardine can. I'm a little guy, and I can barely move around."

Launce said, "This module is a modified Navy DWS, Deep Watch Station. We float them in the abyssal plains to monitor deep-sea activity. Usually, you get three or four guys in here. Not eight. So, it is a bit of a sardine can, isn't it?"

"The SS Sardine," I said.

"Huh, I like that," Launce said. "That's my mother's name, Ardeen. How about it, fellas? The SS Ardeen?"

"You can call it whatever you want," Sal said, "so long

as you get us around safe. I do not intend to become bug splatter just to send a signal to Doris Huntsman."

"I agree," Bel said from Cell Six. "Bellarmine Chichacott. Age fifty-three. Book store owner and former North American chairperson of the International Jeopardy! Foundation. Like Shelton, I devoted my life to preserving knowledge of the old world. But all that came crashing down when my wife died two years ago."

"We're all sorry to hear about that, Bel," Prosper said.

Bel said nothing.

"How about we move on, then? Cell Seven?"

"That's you, Randall," Sal said.

"What?"

"Tell everyone about yourself."

"Hi. My name is Randall Chudleigh. I have two brothers, Rick and Darell, and one sister who died, Terry. And I'm from Gower, Missouri. And my parents are Tim and Joan."

"No offense, but has this guy been declared mentally competent for this mission?" Bel said. "If he needs to be in an institution, it should be in the sunshine of planet Earth."

"They don't want me there," Randall said. "It's all because I—"

Randall told us what he had done, in gruesome detail. From the silence that ensued, I was sure everyone wished he had not.

"That's enough of that, now," Prosper said. "I was just trying to break the ice a little. We've got a long time together with just each other."

I unclenched my butt.

Prosper continued, "How about Cell Eight? It says here your name is Degory Rodriguez. Is that correct?"

Degory typed out a response on the chat bar: *Sí.*

Degory was the one I had seen covered in tattoos, head to toe.

"This guy's got no tongue," Sal said. "I bet he cut it off before the cops had a chance to make him talk. What are you, Degory, Gatos Neros?"

Chantico, he typed.

No one spoke.

Someone cleared his throat.

Even I, who had not spent much time in prison, knew what Chantico was. They were not so much a criminal gang as they were a religious cult. A dark one. Most religions stole from the pockets of the gullible. Chantico drank your blood.

Prepare for launch, came a voice, breaking the long silence.

"Alright, brothers, here we go," Prosper said. "Space or bust."

The voice on the intercom gave a long series of complicated instructions I was sure were not for us—*Confirm depth; Maintain attitude against the current; Engage auto-unlock*—until I heard words I did understand: *Rien ne va plus*. The dealer said that in roulette when the table was spinning. No more bets. I rubbed my thumb along the tattoo on my left hand. I did not want Lady Luck right now. I wanted reality. Something certain. But in the diagram on the computer screen, the rocket was dangling above what looked like a spinning roulette table and was labeled, *Portal Atlantis–I*.

Start propulsion. The can started vibrating.

Pilot module, begin your push.

The vibration increased and moved from the bolts that held the chair down to my spine, to my teeth. We were moving downward again, with force.

Module One clear.

Module Two clear.

Module Three clear.

Release Module One.

Module One released.

The diagram showed Module One being fed into the spinning roulette wheel and disappearing. We were not going up into space at all. We were being fed into a portal at the bottom of the sea.

Module Four clear. Module Two released.

This went on until I felt Module Eight unclasp below my feet.

Pilot module clear.

Release Module Nine, pilot module.

Releasing, either Ash or Willand said. They had not yet spoken to us. *Negative release.*

Release Module Nine, pilot, so we can initiate auto-descend program.

The magnetic locks won't disengage, Atlantis.

After a few seconds of silence, Trenchard said, *Pilot module, return to surface with Module Nine.*

The guys in my module sighed and groaned into the intercom. I put my head back and closed my eyes. We were not going into the portal. We had already failed.

Reversing turbines, Ash and Willand said. *Turbines reversed. Atlantis, confirm depth. We're not rising here.*

You're drifting, pilot.

It's like all our thrust is getting sucked into the portal, and us with it.

Power down, pilot. We'll pull you back up with the comms cable.

Powering down.

The vibration from the turbine stopped, but another vibration, a lower hum, crept upward, starting with my toes.

Atlantis—

Release Module Nine, pilot. Do it now.

A series of deep hums rose from below, making it sound like we were stuck among a pod of whales. I began to see the bright cyan lights of the portal dancing on my window, and I leaned over. It looked like a spiral galaxy. Tiny gray lights like grains of sand rushed by the window. I felt a sudden jolt.

Come in, Atlantis. Come in, Atlantis. Willand, give me comms status.

No comms, Ash. I think the cable snapped.

"What does that mean?" Sal said.

It means if we can't get enough turbine pressure from the pilot module, we're going with you through the portal.

"I'm sure this is all in God's—" Prosper started to say. His stomach must have leapt into his mouth at the same time mine did, like we had suddenly fallen another thousand feet.

We hit something hard. It was completely black outside my window. I turned off the interior light and the computer screen. One by one, white lights began to appear.

"Is that the portal again?" Bel said.

You guys hang tight while Willand and I figure this out.

"They look like stars," Cricket said.

"That they do," Prosper said. "This is good, right, Ash and Willand? We made it into space."

No, it is not. Not good for you and certainly not good for us. Not your module or the pilot module were ever supposed to be in space.

I curled my toes inside my boots. I did not understand what was happening, but I knew things had not gone as planned. Where I could have had a quick and easy execution, now life was uncertain again, open-ended, and messy.

8

"Are we there yet?" Randall asked, and not for the first time.

We had been in space for three hours.

The two Naval officers in the pilot module, Ash and Willand, had been trying to communicate with Atlantis, the base from which we had left, by emergency radio and laser line. They did not seem to be successful and asked us repeatedly to look out our windows for visual contact with Earth.

"No joy," Launce kept saying.

What Ash and Willand did share was the theory the Navy and the IOSS had had: our descent through the portal would bring us directly inside the moonshock. We would skip the four-day journey from Earth's surface to what had become of the moon since the Merge and land directly on another planet. We were never supposed to be in space. Since we were floating in space, though, hope remained that we were somewhere between the Earth and the moonshock.

We were allowed to unbuckle and float around our cells. We had no astronaut training, and none of us could figure out how to go to the bathroom in zero gravity. The IOSS had not expected us ever to be in zero gravity. All that talk about sending us into space had been a way of saying we were going to places *in outer space*, not that we were ever going to travel *through* the vacuum of space to get there.

Nor had the Navy expected their pilot module to stick to Module Nine. Ash and Willand kept trying to release us. I knew this because I kept hearing the light clicking sound of the magnetic locks on the can above my head. They would get rid of us and find their own way home again.

"How is this tuna can even going to keep us alive in space?" Sal said.

"It's built for deep sea pressures," Launce said. "Tight as a drum."

"Our friends upstairs are going to have a problem soon," Bel said. "Each of us has got a year's worth of rations. But those guys are not equipped for this trip."

"That is not our problem," Cricket said. "Let them starve to death, let them experience in a few days what is going to take us a year."

"They are with us now," Prosper said. "For better or for worse. We should help out our brothers."

"I agree," Launce said. "Because so long as the pilot module is attached, we don't have direct control of our own ship. If they die, we're stranded."

Which is why we've got to find a place to land, Ash said. They could hear our conversation though we could not always hear theirs. *I don't suppose they gave you guys spacesuits? The only way to get from your module to ours is through the outside hatch. Another safety feature, I suppose, to keep you guys from sabotaging the mission. Compartmentalization.*

We did not have spacesuits. We had winter coats and work boots.

I looked out the window, at what few stars I could see, and said, "Is there any way to just end it now, you know, abort mission? Blow the reactor or something?"

"I do not accept that," Prosper said. "Let's see what the good Lord has in mind."

"Me neither," Sal said. "If it comes down to it, it comes down to it. But not yet. I've been stuck in worse situations."

Cricket said, "You, sir, have done worse for yourself than floating in the depth of space with no harbor in sight?"

"I once hid in a port-a-john for three hours," Sal said.

"What's so terrible about that?" Cricket said.

"*In* the port-a-john," Sal said. "Shawshank-style."

"That must've been some job," I said.

"Yep," Sal said. "And all I've got to show for the years I put into the business is thirty grand to send my ass away."

"Are we there yet?" Randall said.

Maybe, Willand said. *We're fixing on a possible site. A planet, perhaps, right below us.*

"What kind of planet are we talking about?" Bel said. "There are different kinds of planets."

We're really talking about a photo identification from the cameras on your module. Based on the increase in size over the past few hours, we've got a rough estimate of when we'll get there, in three or four days.

"Hey," I said, "a planet ain't so bad. That's what we want, right?"

We want the kind of land we could see through the portal. Here, we're talking composition unknown. Could be a gas giant. Could be Earth.

"So, it kills us, or it doesn't," Sal said.

"False," Bel said. "It kills us right away, or it slowly suffocates us."

"Either way," Prosper said, "think about this: people will look up into the night sky and realize that we are up there, somewhere. Our bodies will be somewhere, awaiting the resurrection."

"They'll put that on the sympathy card," Bel said. "*I take comfort in knowing that your friend's rotting corpse has made some forgotten nowhere someone's new somewhere.*"

I looked out the window.

"Speaking of rotting corpses," Cricket said, "has anyone tried these High-Density Rations yet? Or even found the ingredients? It says, *For list of ingredients, see box.* But I don't see a box."

"That would be what our friend, Dr. Huntsman, calls 'proprietary,'" Sal said. "As in, 'We don't even know what the hell we ground up in there.' Looks like seaweed packed into a rice cake."

"They come in different flavors," Bel said. "The one I've got tastes a little like gorgonzola."

I said, "I bet it's rat meat. High-Density Rations is a long way of saying 'Hidden Rats.'"

The guys chuckled at this. I felt a smile steal its way onto my lips.

"It's like biting into hard tack, though," Launce said.

No one knew what hard tack was.

"You know, Civil War stuff. Bel, I figured you of all people would know that one. Soldiers used to carry it on their belts. Never went bad."

Prosper said, "It says here to add water, but whenever I

try to squirt water into the little dish they give you, it forms a ball and floats around. Like its own little planet."

"Squirt right onto the rat," Sal said. "That's what I'm doing right now. Soaks right in."

"Right," Prosper said.

I tried that. On the computer screen, though, I saw Degory. Without a word, he was giving us a demonstration. He squeezed water out a bottle into midair, where it formed a ball. He then gently slid a dark green fibrous wafer into the sphere. The High-Density Ration expanded into a round sponge, which he then grabbed and ate. I had already eaten mine without added water, by breaking it into tiny crumbs. The leftover dust from the broken wafer was floating around my cell like they were the stars of their own universe. I would have to wait another six hours before eating another one. There was no list of ingredients on the rice paper wrapper, but there was a stern warning not to eat more than one at a time.

I looked out the window. My belly was full, and space was empty. I wondered if the emptiness of space was another kind of hunger, like the universe had raised us up just to consume us.

***

Six hours passed, during which I took stock of the contents of my cell. In the toolbox, strapped between a multi-bit screwdriver and a hammer, was a six-inch folding knife. We could kill each other at any moment. I had not read anyone's paperwork. What Prosper had said struck me, and I almost regretted telling everyone what I had done. Each of these guys was a killer, I had been sure, one way or another. Maybe Launce had made an "honest mistake," whatever that had meant. Sal was a family man, but I bet he could turn his blood cold when needed. Randall had become a monster, I think, because something had scared him. I could see it in his eyes; they seemed to judge everything as either safe or needing to be crushed. Bel was openly angry. Cricket was quietly angry. I had no idea about Degory. A decision made in the moment had brought each of us here. We had eighty-seven more hours until we reached the planet Ash and Willand thought they had seen. If we made it past that moment, life was going to be a lot harder than it ever had been on Earth. There might be more than one moment in which this knife would make a decision for us.

A bloop came from my computer.

Degory was inviting me to a game of chess.

I clipped the knife onto my belt and sat down.

I knew the basics of chess, but Degory made quick work of me, moving one pawn to bring his queen and bishop into a mating net that took up the whole board. It was over before it began.

I messaged Bel. *You know anything about chess?*

Bel told me he had already played Degory and won. Chess was about establishing careful patterns of attack and defense, not overt aggression, he said. Like in life, those who came out bullying could be deflected, and in deflecting them, a person developed his own pieces into a solid opening. He spent an hour teaching me some basic principles before we both decided we were tired.

I turned off the light in my cell, shut off the computer

monitor, and buckled back into my seat. As bad as it was that we were in space, if I had not chosen to come here, my body would already be in the ground, being eaten by a hungry universe. I fell asleep to Prosper singing gospel songs.

***

I dreamt of Mireille. She was not actually in the dream, but it was all about her. And it was not so much a dream as a couple of images: looking down through green, sunlit trees at the tall white columns of a church facade. Some people were gathered outside, below the branches, where I could not see them, but they seemed happy. It was a wedding, or I interpreted it as a wedding, mine and Mireille's. In real life, we never would have got there. It felt good in dreamland, though.

I turned from looking at the church to what was across the street. The golden sunlight had given way to wintertime, or there were no leaves on the trees—maybe no trees at all—just a bare gray landscape under a thick blanket of dark clouds. It was not foreboding; I was not afraid. Somehow, I still felt the warmth of the white church behind me, radiating through me.

I woke up at six in the morning, Earth time, to my own growling stomach. While I ate my High-Density Ration and drank acrid powdered coffee, I brought to mind my favorite memory of Mireille.

We were in New York, on the upper floor of a skyscraper, while the sun was rising. She was still asleep, turned away from me on her side. We had made the Big Deal the day before and partied into the night. It was quiet. New York had been a quiet city. I watched the sun's golden rays use her neck as a playground. They danced and swung between the loose hairs on her neck the way children use monkey bars. She always kept her hair up so tight, and maybe she had never noticed those few loose hairs. They had been just for me. For one night, anyway.

9

Buckle up, Ash said. *We're coming up on the planet.*

Four days had passed. Ash and Willand had eaten nothing except some energy bars they had had in their uniforms. Terse statements like this were all they could manage. The guys in the can complained about not being able to shower, and that was to say nothing about the gymnastics we had to employ to poop into our floor toilets and keep it there. But Ash and Willand did not complain, at least to us, about having no food or water.

While they slowly starved to death, I learned chess and many other things from Bel. We all learned a little about each other, except Degory, who revealed nothing more than he had the first day. Cricket had been cryptic, too. Sal had not and told us all about his full-time work on the docks in New Jacksonville and his part-time work collecting debts. Launce had found a music app on the computer and composed songs for synthetic instruments, which he accompanied with songs from the Blue Ridge Mountains, some from before the Merge, some from after.

Prepare for reentry.

I had already noticed a light green haze rising below my

window. We were close to the planet. Based on measurements made from our cameras, we could tell it was a gas giant smaller than Jupiter and bigger than Saturn. No one, not even Ash and Willand, could see it directly, and they would not turn the two modules to look. They would not risk missing it. They had used a minimum amount of thrust from our module to steer us directly toward it. Their computer had no software with which to calculate an orbit, and they were Navy sub pilots, not rocket scientists.

Ash and Willand might have been slowly dying over the past four days, but in the next few minutes, we were all going to burn up. *Prepare for reentry*, therefore, had meant "Prepare to die."

We had been preparing, in different ways. I sketched the faces of my module mates from what I could see on the computer and from what I remembered of them at the warehouse in Atlantis. Prosper sang and prayed. Launce sang plaintive bluegrass songs. Sal and Bel competed for who could contrive the most outlandish death scenario. Bel's descriptions of metal rain and melting skin had sounded drawn from science fiction books. Sal's descriptions of more precise tortures at the hands of our alien hosts had likely come from real-world experience.

"We never named her," Cricket said. "We should name the planet that's going to melt us from the inside out."

"Hope," Prosper said.

"Too ironic," Bel said.

"That's too many syllables," I said. "No planet has that many syllables. Think about it: Earth. Mars. Venus's got two.

You get three, max: Jupiter. Mercury. Too Ironic has four. That's too many."

Bel snickered. I had missed something.

"Hope," Prosper said. "One syllable says it all."

I rubbed the tattoo on my left hand. That woman had a name, but I was not sure it was important. "Doris," I said. "She's the one who got us into this mess. Planet Doris."

Ash and Willand laughed, weakly. I had redeemed myself after whatever Bel had laughed at.

"I like it," Sal said. "If we survive this, somehow, we'll name it something else. Until then, it's that witch's cauldron."

"She was nice," I said, immediately regretting it.

"Oh, yeah?" Sal said. "How nice are we talking here?"

"Man, I just mean she talked to me before I got into this sardine can."

"What did she say?" Cricket said.

"I don't remember," I said. "Couldn't have been important."

"Important enough for you to think she was nice," Launce said.

"Hey, I don't want to spend my last breath talking about Doris Huntsman," I said.

"Then tell us about Mireille," Sal said with a more serious, fatherly tone.

I sighed. "I don't want to spend my last minutes thinking about her, neither."

"Nor I," Bel said. "Let's just have some silence."

I brought my mother's face to mind, and all the happy memories I had of her, and that girly smile she had, even in the hospital wrapped in rubber tubes, even when there was nothing left of her except skin and bones.

The light green haze filled my cell. Planet Doris's horizon rose into view. The gas giant had broad bands of blue, green, and gold.

The module began to vibrate. Bel had reminded us, many times, that we had no heat shield. We would burn up before the pressure of the planet ever crushed our lungs.

My butt lifted off the seat, and my shoulders pressed hard against the harness while my feet held firm against the floor. It was like I was being stretched in two directions.

This is unexpected, Ash said. *We see a white haze above our module. Can any of you confirm that from below?*

I tried to contort my body to see through the upper part of the window.

"No joy," Launce said. "Wait…."

The white haze fell below the top of the window. The once endless expanse of black was becoming a thinner and thinner line between the blue-green haze of the planet below us and whatever was clamping down on us from above.

My body stretched harder in both directions. The can's vibration was threatening to shake my bones into a pile of rocks.

Prepare for entry, Ash said, but it looked like we were pulling away from the planet.

A gargled sound came through the intercom, then a loud pop shook the whole module. Nothing but white light filled the window.

"Is this heaven yet?" I said, hoping Prosper would hear.

But my more immediate concern was the seat restraint, digging into my lap and shoulders. "Are we upside down?"

"Yes," Prosper said.

"Are we rolling?" Bel said.

"Negative," Launce said. "Ash and Willand, what do you see?"

No answer came.

"Come in, pilot module." When no one answered, Launce said, "I've got no controls here. We've gone ballistic, and I don't even know what's up or down anymore."

"Hope," Prosper said.

"The computer knows what we're in, though," Bel said, his voice straining. "Hydrogen. Almost pure hydrogen."

"Is that, what, is that good or bad?" Sal said.

"It's fire," Bel said. "Wait. It's changing. Increasing oxygen levels."

The module shook.

"We hit a new layer," Launce said. "And I see what Bel sees now. Oxygen's denser than hydrogen. The atmosphere's layered. Hey, what's this button do? *Correct attitude?* Yes, ma'am."

I saw the flashing button on the computer screen, too. It disappeared. My body slammed against the straps into the cell. My butt was firm in the seat again. We were right side up.

Outside the window, the white haze was streaked with a thin line of orange and red.

"Fire!" Bel said. "The atmosphere's on fire."

I stared out the window at how I was going to die. Four streaks of fire flew out from the engines underneath us and spiraled far into the distance. But they did not billow out into some great explosion. We were not melting.

Instead, the spiral arms of flame grew wider, and at the center of each one emerged a dark blue-black line. The spirals of fire thickened until the blue-black lines were like tree trunks around which fire clung like ivy. Those tree trunks widened until they grew into each other. The ivy of fire dissolved. The sky was completely black.

While I waited for something else to happen, I pressed my hand to the window. It was cold.

The lights went out in my cell. The computer went blank. If anyone was saying anything, I could not hear it.

After a few minutes of hearing nothing but my own breath and feeling no forces on the module—no vibrating, no shaking, no clicking, no popping—the bottom of the module slammed into something. We had hit at an angle, and after a few seconds, the other side of the module hit. The can spun on its bottom ring like a coin on the counter until it stopped.

After another few minutes of hearing nothing but my own heartbeat and feeling the module begin to slide across the ground, the lights and the computer came back on. Before I could say anything into the intercom, I heard a whoosh from below my feet.

Hull inflated, came a message on the screen.

"Hull?" Bel said. "Hulls are for boats."

"Yes, they are," Launce said. "Yes, they are. Bel, do you find a depth reading anywhere?"

"You mean altitude?"

"No, I believe I mean depth. Look outside. This is what the deep dark ocean looks like."

10

Over the course of an hour, the chilly blackness outside my window gave way to midnight blue. The module, which Launce kept calling the Ardeen, gently swayed as it rose to the surface. We would not know how deep the ocean was until we broke the surface. That came, all at once, seventy-two minutes into our ascent.

Bright white light poured into my window, searing my eyes for a few seconds. While I recovered, hoots and cheers came from the other guys through the intercom.

Silver-crested waves slapped against the side of the can. The sky was an inarticulate white haze.

Ash and Willand did not respond to Launce's calls or knocking.

The ocean was four hundred feet deep.

"That means we're relatively close to shore," Launce said. "If the Azores, real close. If North America, a few tens of miles. Either way, I'm sure the Navy will pick us up now."

I pulled my head back. No part of me had thought we would come back up through the portal.

"You're sure we're back on Earth?" Sal said, reading my mind.

"Where else could we be?"

"Planet Doris," I said. "Hope. Too Ironic. Whatever you want to call it."

"I'm starting to agree with Launce on this," Bel said. "The pressures of a planet the size of the one we approached, that's no good for oceans, atmosphere."

"We were pulling away from Planet Hope," Prosper said. "This is somewhere else."

"Check the atmosphere," Sal said. "That'll tell us where we are. You guys know where all that is on this computer."

I had found the menu but did not know how to interpret the information.

"That's…hold on," Launce said. "Bel, what do you think? Pretty close, right?"

"Close, but not exactly the air we left. Higher oxygen levels, lower carbon dioxide—almost no carbon dioxide. Some nitrogen. Trace gases. That's not quite Earth."

I said, "Look, I don't want to sound stupid or nothing, but is the air the same everywhere on Earth? I mean, looking at the temperature outside, we maybe came up in the deep winter somewhere. Antarctica or Russia."

"What about the fact that we set the air on fire?" Sal said. "Let's not forget that."

"Are we alright?" Randall said.

"Yeah, Randall, we're alright. Wherever we are, we're fine."

"What does that mean?" Randall said.

"It means we're either back on Earth or on a new planet, where we can live."

"We are alive," Prosper said. "Thank the good Lord."

"That we are," Launce said. "But we're still trapped in the Ardeen until we can detach the pilot module. If we're on Earth, it's no problem. Someone will help us from the outside. But if not, we've got to do it ourselves."

"So, now you're back to ifs and maybes?" Sal said.

"Hey, it doesn't matter," I said. "We've got to float here and wait. Ash and Willand told us we couldn't get into their module. Safety precautions and all."

"Not from space," Launce said. "But Bel and I have been studying the issue. In fact, you may be the one to help us."

"Me? How?"

Launce explained: our floor toilet unit dropped into a trough that circled the core of the module. In order to vent the toilets away from our cells, a fan drew fresh air along the trough and into a filtration unit. That unit was accessible from two places: the vestibule and my cell.

"So, what exactly are you saying to me?"

"If you remove the fan and filter unit, you can get into the vestibule. From there, you can get outside. Once outside, you can get up to the pilot module."

"Can anyone even fit down there?" I said.

"It's twenty inches wide, ten deep," Launce said. "You're just going to have to give it a shot."

"What about Degory? He's right next to the vestibule, too."

"Let's be honest," Sal said. "You're small enough."

"Degory's as skinny as I am."

"But you, how do you say this...," Launce said.

"You speak English," Sal said. "Hell, you can talk at all."

"The man's got a point," Prosper said. "We need every advantage."

"It comes down to two candidates," Cricket said. "And we all vote for you."

"So, what, this is democracy?" I said. "Voting on who's going to crawl through the sewer for you?"

"With you next to the vestibule," Prosper said, "I would say the good Lord has chosen you for this role."

"It wasn't God, it was Doris Huntsman," I said.

"Well, prove the good woman right," Cricket said. "Who knows, maybe you'll impress her in the end."

"Would y'all just stop about Doris Huntsman?" I said. "It isn't like that."

"You're the one who brought her into this," Sal said. "And you're not helping yourself by saying, 'It ain't like that.' No one would have thought it was like that until you said it wasn't."

"Y'all are incredible," I said. I rubbed my face with my hands.

I could hear the guys snickering through the intercom.

"Okay, hold on," I said. "Let's count up all the factors here. Once I get through, then what? It's cold outside. I won't fit through with my winter gear on. And probably not my boots, neither. And the waves are splashing up at us. I'm going to get wet. And that's to say nothing about sliding next to the reactor core, which they told us not to hang around next to."

"You'd be taking one for the team," Launce said. "We'll talk you through it."

"I think you keep proving you're the right man for the

job," Bel said. "You see the whole process already, beginning to end."

"All I did was list six ways this will kill me."

"Well, not unlike military testing," Launce said.

"I can't believe you guys."

"But we believe in you," Cricket said.

Yo también, Degory wrote.

"Yeah," I said. "Because you don't gotta do it."

I unbuckled my belt and bent over to untie my boots.

Launce and Bel guided me through the process: I lifted up the panel of the floor toilet like I normally would, this time on my knees, where the whiff of four days' worth of poop ran right up my nose. I felt under the rim of the opening for a latch that would lift up a larger panel. A whole section of the floor came up. With this set aside, I turned the four screws that held the litter box in place. It had a handle on one end for carrying through the upper hatch so we could use our poop as fertilizer. I picked this up and set it inside my cell. I peered into the trough: toward the vestibule, I saw a gray metal box. I heard the fan whirring. I could not reach it from within my cell.

I shined a flashlight to see what kind of tools I would need to disassemble the fan-filter unit: the multi-bit screwdriver and, for backup, folding pocket pliers.

I sized myself against the hole the toilet unit left behind. It would take some serious gymnastics to insert myself, arms ahead of me. I tried six different ways and took a break, out of breath. Finally, I found a way to roll in, and my back hit hard against the floor of the trough.

My tools were already ahead of me, toward the fan unit.

There would have been no way to reach the pockets of my jumpsuit once my arms were ahead of me, deep into the shaft. I pulled myself forward, into the darkness.

The flashlight did not help as much as feeling for the nuts that held the unit in place, so I turned it off. My body blocked most of the light coming from my cell. Where the walls, floor, and ceiling of the shaft did not squeeze me, the stench of seven toilets washed over me. I yelled loudly about this, for everyone to hear from their toilets.

Sal yelled back, "You've seen *Shawshank*. It could've been worse. Hell, I know it personally."

While I was reaching for the pliers, I felt a fold of metal like the latch I had used to free the floorboard. It pulled. The fan unit pushed ahead on a hinge, into the vestibule. I would not have to turn any nuts or screws.

My boots and winter coat were tied to my ankles with the rope I might need to climb up to the pilot module. I pulled myself forward, into the dark vestibule. My coat-and-boots combo snagged, and it took five minutes to push myself back in and kick them loose. Finally, I was on the floor of the vestibule. Lights clicked on automatically.

Sal, who had suggested tying the extra gear to my ankles, had also suggested I not wear the insulated pants they had given us. The splashing waves would soak them and weigh me down. So, in work boots, thin synthetic jumpsuit, and with the hood of the winter coat pulled over my head, I opened the vestibule door to the air of a new world.

A thousand tiny knives of ice tore at my throat and lungs. I pulled the door closed again.

"Yo, it is butt-ass cold out there," I said, into the vestibule intercom.

"Tie a handkerchief around over your mouth," Launce said. "Congratulations, by the way. You're the first one out there."

"Handkerchief, handkerchief," I said, patting my coat and pants pockets. I had nothing but the socks on my feet to use, and I tied them across my nose and mouth.

With the door fully open, I saw the rolling ocean crash against the yellow inflatable hull a few feet below. The door, conveniently, had a ladder on the inside. I closed and re-opened it, this time clinging to the ladder. It latched magnetically to the outside of the can, but the hold was not strong enough for the biggest beatdowns the sea gave, and I flopped back and forth a few times. Looking up at the pilot module, I could see its four turbines burnt and broken. The nose cone was slightly melted.

I took the rope, tied it into a noose, and tossed it, after many tries, over the nose cone. It slid off as soon as I pulled. Waves were biting at my feet. The water was very warm in itself, but the frigid air turned my ankles into icicles. After what felt like an hour, and what was probably ten minutes, I lassoed one of the turbines. It held.

Being a welterweight had its advantages, and I had no problem pulling myself onto the rim of Module Nine. I tied the rope around my waist. The hatch to the pilot module was on the other side. I shimmied along the rim and tried manually to release the magnetic locks connecting the two modules. They would not budge.

Through the windows of the pilot module, all I saw was

black. We had dived nose first into this atmosphere, and the pilot module had served as a heat shield. I did not expect to find Ash and Willand alive inside.

I turned the handle and opened the hatch. Black water poured out. Death clawed at my nose.

I stepped into the pilot module, into a shallow swamp. Light seeped through a small crack above my head. Ash and Willand were pale and puffy. Their skin was breaking open. They had not burned up and had probably drowned in the ocean. But they had been alive only an hour ago. No one could decay that fast.

None of the many buttons I saw turned the electricity back on. Based on Launce's instructions, I looked for a breaker panel. It took another ten minutes to find. I flipped every breaker until one was left, marked *Main*. I flipped it off. I felt a solid click come up through my feet.

A few seconds later, the module began to ascend. Launce had taken control. I could feel knocking through the floor. The guys were congratulating me. I knocked back.

Launce took us a few hundred feet in the air and spun us slowly. He had us looking for a place to go. As soon as the thin white line of a snowy shore came into view, Launce took us in that direction.

The wind pushed the pilot module half an inch off the ring of our module, and it crashed down again. Launce must have felt this, too, because we stopped. But we went forward again, more slowly. I stood in three inches of death water, my hands gripped the sides of the hatch, and the icy wind ripped at my face. I would rather endure the pain of watching through the wind a strange new shore come into view than to look back at the rotting corpses of the men that had brought us here.

11

The thin white line we had seen was the edge of a free-floating ice sheet. We landed there, on the yellow inflatable hull. I climbed back into the vestibule of Module Nine.

"What you tell me about the pilot module coming loose during flight is what I felt," Launce said, through the intercom. "It's not safe to fly any farther like that."

"We can pull it off. I've got a rope on it."

Launce took a second and said, "We risk bending the rim of the Ardeen, if not breaking it. That's our tent in there, in that ring. Come back through to your cell and close up the fan. It's starting to stink in here."

I looked at the tiny shaft through which I had climbed an hour ago.

"Look, I'd rather not, alright? Can I just ride it out here?"

"There's nowhere to strap in, Keyes. And I've got to maneuver this thing so I can safely cast off the pilot module. You get what I'm saying?"

Prosper said, "I hope you're not talking about dumping the bodies of those two men at sea."

"I'm talking about dumping the pilot module, Prosper. Their bodies just happen to be inside. There's no other way."

"Those men died bringing us here," Prosper said. "They nearly starved to death before they got burned and drowned. We owe them a proper burial. You're in the Navy, Launce. Think about how you'd want to be treated."

I heard only breathing through the intercom.

"We've got to have some principles," Sal said.

"Hold on now," I said. "What exactly does 'principles' mean here? It means I'm doing something while y'all sit in your cells."

Bel said, "I'm thinking about that first module, those guys who volunteered to take the dead body with them. They had principles. Do we have body bags?"

"One for each of us," Sal said. "At the bottom of our trunks. Biodegradable."

"So, maybe Ash and Willand don't die in vain," Bel said. "We find a place to bury them, give new life to this place."

"Which might still be Earth," I said.

"Doubtful," Launce said.

"I think all their nutrients washed out in the black water," I said, fairly certain that was untrue. "It's too late for them."

"Sal's right," Cricket said. "We've got to set standards for our behavior here. This is our world now."

"Principles. Standards. Democracy," I said. "That's me crawling through the toilet and putting two squishy-ass corpses into body bags while you sit in your cells and ponder the mysteries of the universe."

"Prosper and I can slide our body bags to you along the shaft," Sal said. "You don't have to crawl in to get yours."

"Thank God for small favors," I said.

***

I tucked the body bags into my jumpsuit and climbed back up to the pilot module. This was all easier now that we were on an ice floe, but the sheet was shrinking. The warm water was melting it.

A thin layer of ice had formed on the water left in the pilot module. This made it easier to lay out the body bags for Ash and Willand. Their buckles were frozen to their bodies, and I tore Ash's flight suit. He had been wearing a Star of David underneath. Their nearly frozen bodies did not bend, but the body bags did, and I dragged each bundle of death to the hatch, tied it to the rope, and let it drop. I pushed the rope alongside the edge of the can. It pleased me to think that their bodies were passing by the windows on the module below, and I made sure to walk each body a different way, so everyone had a view of what I was doing. When the body bag hung in front of the vestibule, I climbed down and pulled it inside. For a man of my size, five-six and one-thirty-one, this was not easy.

Once both bags were in, I did not want to lose the rope, so I cut it as close as I could to the turbine to which I had tied it. I climbed back into the vestibule, which now had two bodies in it. I closed the hatch, took off my boots and winter coat, and stuffed them ahead of me in the toilet trough. This time, though, I tied the rope to the fan unit, so all I had to do was pull it closed from my cell.

With my toilet unit screwed back in place, and after scrubbing myself several times with alcohol wipes, I strapped back into my seat.

"Done," I said.

"Good," Launce said. "By the look of things outside, we're almost out of ice. Hang on, guys. This might get messy."

While I had been pulling rotting flesh out of the attic, Launce had been busy figuring out the best way to lose the pilot module. The Ardeen would not let us do a loop or a roll. It would, though, in Launce's cryptic words, "get out of its own way."

This meant hovering to a few thousand feet above sea level and letting the module drop. While it dropped, he would ignite one side engine. A little gravity and a lot of counter thrust would generate the roll we needed.

At ten thousand feet, all I could see was white haze. The module's hover tech engines stopped humming. My stomach flew into my throat. We were in free fall. When we picked up enough speed, one engine kicked in, and my head flew sideways, into my cell. I heard the two bodies in the vestibule hit the ceiling. My arms fell past my head. We were upside down. I did not hear the pilot module fall away from us, but I did hear the two bodies in the vestibule hit the wall and then the floor. A green light went on next to my upper hatch. We were upright again, I knew, because all of my bones dug like pikes into my seat.

"Success," Launce said. "We're free and clear."

The guys cheered.

"But that stunt cost us a lot of battery life. We're going to have to float it out for a while until the reactor recharges the batteries."

***

The eight of us sat on the edge of our open cell hatches, on the roof of Module Nine, wearing our winter clothes.

The wind was biting cold, but whenever it stopped, warmth radiated upward from the sea. We were seeing each other in the flesh for the first time in over four days.

"And smelling each other, too," Cricket said. "It's been four days without a shower."

Launce looked behind him, toward the water. "You say the water's warm, Keyes?"

"Like a hot tub."

"It's cold up here, though," Bel said.

"Hang on. I've got something for that," Sal said.

He came back half a minute later with a bottle of whisky.

"Hot damn," Launce said. "Where'd you get that?"

"Let's just say it's my business to know people who get things." He drank and passed the bottle to Prosper.

Prosper took a careful sip and handed the bottle to me.

I studied the label. "This is top shelf, Sal. Trust me, I know."

"Oh, you know?" Sal said.

"It's my business, as a collector, to know." I took a swig and leaned across the vestibule hatch to hand the bottle to Degory. "You wouldn't believe what's left behind up there."

"Hey, don't be giving Keyes a hard time," Launce said. "Look what the young man did for us."

"Cheers," said Bel, who now had the bottle, after Degory and Randall had drunk. The guys echoed him.

"Yeah, whatever," I said. "I'm tired."

"Not 'whatever,'" Bel said.

"It would've been whoever was next to the toilet fan."

"No, none of us could've done it. Saved our lives, practically," Launce said, and he drank from the bottle.

He handed it to Cricket, who muttered something about being clean for three years before handing it on to Sal.

"Look, I'm tired and don't want to talk about it, alright?"

"First time seeing a dead body?" Sal said after he drank.

"It's not about the bodies," I said. "Just leave it alone. I did what I did."

I took the bottle and drank as deeply as I could. Everyone's eyes were on me.

Degory passed the bottle along to Randall without drinking. Randall looked to Sal for approval, who gave it. Bel wiped the rim of the bottle after Randall drank and spilled a little on his coat.

"It's just the same kind of situation that got me here in the first place," I said. "But I don't want to talk about it."

"That's fair," Prosper said, next to me. "But tell me about those tattoos you got on your hands."

"That's easy," I said. "On my right, you've got the crossed keys. Skeleton keys for Shelton Keyes. Simple as that. Those came first. But this," I held up my left hand, "this is special. This is my symbol for reality. It looks like a lock, right, but if you look carefully, it's in the shape of a woman wearing a long dress, a gown, you know, with the hood up and everything. I'll tell you where I saw her, and you'll understand a bit about my truth as a collector. Y'all listening?"

The guys nodded. Some guys smirked.

"Alright. So, I do my work in the Safe Zone, which is what you call a paradox, a contradiction in terms."

"An oxymoron," Bel said.

"Gesundheit," Sal said.

"North of forty latitude, it is neither safe nor a clearly

defined zone. But the Collector Laws give us free rein. And it is a reign, we like to say, a kingdom of our own, where a lot of the reality y'all don't see is kept secret, tucked away. You want stuff from the old world, but a collector has got to revisit that world to get it for you, under threat of long, deadly summers and longer, deadlier winters. I mean, it's like human beings were all diseased back then, in the head, you know, the way they kept piling up stuff in their houses.

"And it was worst in New York. That's where it all came to me, reality. These old skyscrapers, people living in tinier and tinier apartments in taller and taller buildings, for no reason that makes sense to me. Did you know there are still thousands of people living there? They're all huddled up in walled neighborhoods. And around St. Patrick's Cathedral, it's a whole 'nother show. They're in there praying all day—no offense, Prosper—like they're going to bring the old world back to life again.

"But maybe there's something to that, I'm thinking. I'm in New York on an invite from upper echelon people—you've gotta have an in to collect in New York—and we're at this church, like I said. Outside, across the street, there's a great big bronze statue of Atlas holding up the world. But it's not the world, it's a few intersecting circles of metal your mind makes into a globe. And it's all covered in ivy now. The guy's legs are bent, you see him struggling to pick up the globe on his shoulders.

"Inside, deep inside the church, all the way in the back, there's a lady made of white marble. She's also holding a globe, but a small one, made out of stone, right in her hands, at her waist. She's smiling, not struggling. That, to me, is reality. That's dealing with reality. Not big old abstract ideas, like Atlas. You just take a bit of earth as it comes. People got ideas back then, weird ones, and you see all that being ground away by glaciers right now. But reality is kept up by a few people living together. That's what's on my left hand, gentlemen. A reminder to deal with reality. Not ideas."

"I appreciate you, Shelton, I really do," Prosper said. "But perhaps you might consider a little of what you said. Those people who were taking care of things, an idea brought them together. A lot of these guys, all these guys, I bet, myself included, got too much reality, up close and too soon. Some good ideas might've kept us from death row."

"I hear you," I said.

"All I'm saying is what you said: you saw a statue of a bad idea and a statue of a good idea, two ways of dealing with the same reality."

I looked for the bottle, which Sal had in his hands.

"Alright, it is definitely too cold out here now," Bel said.

"First, let's do right by Ash and Willand," Launce said.

He and Prosper brought the two bodies to the top of the module and laid them side by side. The sea was calm enough for us to stand without falling over, but Prosper suggested we stand in a circle and put our arms across each other's shoulders. This kept us a lot more stable. Launce made his commendations, and Prosper sang. Sal muttered something and made the Sign of the Cross. When I told him Ash was Jewish, he said, "So was Jesus." Bel insisted on opening their bags, just enough to see their faces, so he could stick a ration wafer into each of their mouths. "Charon's obol," he said. "To pay for their journey across the Styx." When I repeated my discovery that Ash was Jewish and suggested that Willand might not be a pagan, either, Bel said, "To make it worth it, their death. If they've died here, they'll want to have given life to this planet, like the rest of us. These rations pack a lot of life in them, probiotics." He zipped up the bags again. Launce and Prosper tossed Willand overboard. Randall insisted he get to swing Ash over, and Sal took the other end.

Back in my cell, where it was warm, I looked at the tattoo on my left hand and rubbed it with my thumb. We had just faced the reality of death with a few strange ideas, and I was not sure it was so bad.

12

By sunset, this new planet had convinced us it was not Earth. First of all, we did not see the sun set. It took twenty hours after we buried Ash and Willand for the blinding white mist we called "day" to turn into black-hole darkness. The batteries had slowly recharged during that time, but no one thought it worth flying in the dark. We had, though, thought it worth taking baths in the ocean during the day, and guys tied themselves by rope to the vestibule door so they could bathe in private and not worry about being washed away at sea. The baths were quick: the water was warm, almost too warm for comfort, and none of us knew what kinds of exotic sea life lurked in the depths or what strange compound in the water might melt our skin off. The water was not salty, and it was also not tasty, smelling a bit like sulfur.

Before dark, we erected the dome tent. That was easy. All we had to do was pull one half of the ring that lined the top of the module up, over, and across to the other side. The tent pulled with it, a dome of fabric lined with stabilizing ribs, spanning the width of the can. We pulled sleeping bags from our cells up to the module roof, now under the dome tent, and slept with our feet at the center. There was no radiation warning on this level.

I slept with the six-inch folding knife under my pillow. It was not that I thought any one of the other guys was such a psychopath he would kill for the fun of it. It was that I never knew what I should or should not say to them, how I might already have offended them. Except for Bel and Launce, they all seemed like professional criminals, seasoned prisoners. They could make an example out of me, especially when they grew tired of eating Hidden Rats, the name we had given to our High-Density Rations.

I woke up frequently, unable to see who else was awake, who might be standing over me. Bel snored terribly, and when Launce finally convinced him to turn onto his side, Bel farted. We all laughed. I loosened my grip on the knife a little.

Eight hours after sunset, we were all awake again, wondering what to do in the dark, wondering when the sun would rise. After twenty hours had passed, the amount of daylight we had had yesterday, we started to worry. That first night lasted thirty-six hours.

So did the next day. We took down the tent so we could fly again and hovered over the sea for five hours. This was the maximum the batteries would allow at peak efficiency, which the computer had given as a rule called "forty over four": forty miles an hour at four hundred feet above ground. Like on Earth, hover tech was convenient, but it was not powerful. You still had to burn dead dinosaurs for speed. Launce said it was good not to go so fast, anyway, considering our limited visibility. A system of lasers called "lidar" made a three-dimensional map of the terrain as we flew, but all that meant, over the endless ocean, was a squiggly blur below us. We floated on that choppy sea while we waited to recharge. Some guys fished with lines and lures the IOSS had given us. Nothing bit.

Days passed this way. We developed a rhythm. During daylight, it was wake—sleep—wake, and during the night it was sleep—wake—sleep. Bel called this a "checkerboard day."

Launce taught each of us how to fly the can. We all did fine, more or less. None of us had known Randall before this, but we could not imagine he had ever had a bigger joy in his life than what he showed at flying the can, and he kept laughing in spurts for hours. It was infectious, his joy, and the big man's spirit carried us through the long days and long nights. That, and reading on our own through the computer endless encyclopedia entries about life on Earth; playing games of chess, poker, and pinochle; and studying instructions for planting the seeds we had with us and the best kinds of places to bury our own bodies on this new planet.

After a week at sea, Earth time, the water started to become even warmer. The air was still frigid. The waves calmed, or at least became less chaotic, as much as we could see them through the thickening mist. Every few hours, the module made a strange motion on the water, like it had been knocked by a whale. This would roll us into each other during sleep, so much that some guys preferred to sleep strapped into their seats in their cells below and not under the dome tent above. I had enough room to curl on the floor of my cell. In that position, one night, I was the last to feel us spinning.

"It's a whirlpool," I heard Bel say, from above. My hatch was closed. I heard the stomping of feet and the yelling of guys to pull down the tent, throw the sleeping bags into the cells, batten down the hatches, and brace for impact. A quick roll call told us we were all safely in our cells by the time the whirlpool had submerged the module.

We spun counterclockwise, pressing me against my straps and casting my arms and legs in front of me. I saw only black through the window. Just as quickly as the maelstrom had started, it stopped again, and we resurfaced.

"One hundred and fifteen degrees," Launce said. "That's a warm bath we're in."

"Too warm for an ocean," Bel said. "Especially one that's four hundred feet deep."

Volcanes, Degory wrote. *La mujer.*

"He might be right, scientifically," Bel said. "Theologically, that's another story."

"Right, Prosper?" I said.

"No comment," Prosper said.

No comment was probably the right answer, so long as we were stuck in the same can as the volcano-worshipping Degory.

***

At sunrise I saw, through the mist, a black disc on the northeastern horizon.

"It's the portal we came through," Prosper said.

"It's a moon being eclipsed," Bel said. "Our planet's got a moon. A big one."

"It's progress," Launce said. "The only way we have of measuring that we've covered any distance at all. Because the depth of the ocean has not changed one bit. Not after traveling eight thousand miles. I say we make getting below that moon our target."

Everyone agreed. We had no choice on a planet that had showed us nothing but water. Anything different was progress.

Day by day, that silhouetted slice of a moon grew taller, and the moon took shape, spreading its black wings wider and wider across the horizon. This meant we were coming closer.

During those same days, many more whirlpools formed. We flew over them when we had battery, and when we did not, we slept strapped into our cells at night, with the dome tent pulled back down into the rim of the module. This was an irritating routine, but when we woke up underwater, as we sometimes did because of the whirlpools, dry inside our sealed cells and not drowned in the boiling sea, our complaints went away.

As the hot water warmed the air, strong winds formed waterspouts, dozens of them per day, as far as we could see. The wind drove away the mist.

"This is creation at work," Prosper said. We were all strapped into our cells, hearing each other through the intercom. "Gentlemen, we are living a genesis moment. Nature is finding a new balance in our presence. First, we separated water from atmosphere. Now, the atmosphere is separating into air and clouds."

Bel stroked his chin.

"You believe this, Bel?" I said.

He tapped his chin. "I would express it differently, but Prosper may be on to something."

Soon after this, the tsunamis started. They were only a few feet tall, but they were fast. They were more annoying than dangerous, but they did wipe out the whirlpools. They always came from the same direction: the black moon rising to the northeast.

After the fourth tsunami of the day, I said to Prosper, "Explain the genesis of that."

"Tidal forces," Bel said. "That's simple enough. The moon is probably locked in a stationary orbit around our planet. It's probably bouncing up and down just a little, just a fraction of a fraction, like a bobber."

"A fraction of a what?" Launce said.

Bel did not answer. He knew many things as past president of the Jeopardy! Foundation, but he was not a scientist.

"How about that moon send us down some more whisky?" I said. "Or real food. I'm tired of eating vegetable crackers."

"Don't even start on that," Cricket said. "No talk about food. Not now. First of all, you're just gonna make me hungry enough to eat one of you, but you don't have to worry about that because I can barely hold down my rats because of all this rocking at sea."

"Alright, Hannibal Lecter. How about we give this planet a real name," Sal said. "Tornado Land."

"Yeah, that's a real name," Cricket said.

"Hope," Prosper said. "Straight and clear."

"New Earth," I said.

"What has the old Earth ever done for us?" Launce said. "Let's leave all that behind. I say we go completely original."

"Dorisland," Cricket said. "That's what Shelton says in his sleep."

"Enough, y'all," I said.

"Elpis," Bel said. "That's hope in Greek."

"Sounds science-fictiony," Launce said.

No one answered. I heard a faint sound like a cannon going off in the distance.

"Did something fall?" Launce said.

No one answered.

A tsunami hit us a few hours later.

***

"Land ho," Cricket said after four weeks at sea.

In that time, the moon had risen high enough—that is, we had come underneath it—that it was totally off the horizon, a complete circle. We only saw it during the daily eclipse, when the sun passed behind it, as a dark silhouette behind the clouds. The daily eclipse lasted three hours. The clouds had never parted, not once in four weeks.

Also in that time, we heard more bursts in the air. They usually came with a tsunami.

Cricket was right. A thin gray line appeared on the horizon one morning while I was flying the can. We flew toward it for hours without seeming to make any progress. Just as I was about to set the module down on the sea, I heard Cricket yelling.

"Up, up, up! Shelton, now!"

I pushed us up a few hundred feet. Before Cricket could explain, a burst nearly broke my eardrums.

"Rogue wave," Cricket said. "Hundreds of feet high. Nearly got us."

"Megatsunami," Launce said.

"The devil's trying to hold us back," Prosper said.

"Can I set this thing down now?" I said.

"Not yet," Launce said. "More are sure to follow."

"I tell you what, though," Cricket said. "The coast is a lot closer now."

I turned the can to see. We had made no progress for hours, and suddenly a wall of light gray rock loomed ahead.

"I've got to land us now," I said. "Battery's down. *No más.*"

While we recharged, we floated away from the mountainous coast.

"I don't like this," Launce said. "Those tsunamis could be caused by landslides."

"This planet's been trying to eat us since we got here," Sal said. "Fire, floods, whirlpools, tsunamis, you name it."

"But it hasn't got us yet," Prosper said. "Don't you see? We're in the right place. We're well equipped with this little tuna can and a big helping of God's grace. Besides, where are we going to go? We've got to wait it out. So far, so good."

We could not tell how tall the mountain range was because clouds billowed against it at least ten thousand feet above us. Rain from those clouds splashed down its face, which was too steep to land on. We saw no trees, no grass, nothing to indicate life. It was a wall of smooth gray rock, slowly undulating on its way toward the northern and southern horizons.

"Even if we could get up there now, fully charged,"

Launce said, "we won't get to ten thousand feet vertical before we need to recharge again. And I don't see any place to land up there. We'll have to pick a direction and look for a gap."

"I say north," Sal said.

"Which way is north?" Cricket said.

I cocked my head at him. "The place it always is. To the left of the rising sun."

"Yes, but we don't know that the sun doesn't rise in the west here."

"Are you serious?" I said. "That is the very definition of east: where the sun rises."

Cricket stitched together a tight smile. He was talking just for the sake of getting a rise out of someone. It worked, on me.

"You're making me tired," Bel said. "We go north, toward the equator, where it's bound to be warmer, until we find a way in."

The mood picked up again as we all poked our heads through our hatches to scan the mountainside for a gap we could enter or a flat area on which we could land.

Then, during the second flight of that first day near land, thirty-three days into our voyage, our new world opened up to us. It was a fjord, Bel explained. It was about half a mile wide, and the near-vertical walls stretched past the cloud layer two miles above us. It was clay-colored rock, a mute gray, with an occasional seam of deep sparkling blue.

The continent opened to us, and it opened deeply. We hovered into the fjord for over an hour, and nothing about its appearance changed. That was over forty miles with no ground on which to land. We were still water-bound.

"Man, she's not gonna give herself up so easy, is she?" Launce said, after twenty minutes of total silence.

"She's a she?" Prosper said.

"Who else would make an easy promise like this and then make you work your butt off for it?" Launce said.

I thought of Mireille's neck. Mireille had made me work for it, and I had. In the end, though, maybe she had felt she had not made me work hard enough and had regretted it.

I looked around at the other guys. They said nothing and stared blankly at the walls of dull gray rock. We were in our new world now, and the answer to Launce's question—the women in our lives—would only live as ever-distant memories.

PART THREE

PLANT

13

Not far along after Launce's comment about the unforgiving canyon, it split into two channels. To one side, it continued straight, tall, and formidable. To the other, it was narrow, twisting, and unstable. Between the two channels, the rock had crumbled, carving away a few steps on its way into the clouds.

"I hereby dub this place the Stairway to Heaven," Launce said. He typed the name into the three-dimensional computer map and flew us upward, to the flattest step we could find before the battery gave out. There would be just enough room outside the module for us to stand around, especially when Launce deflated the hull and the can rested on its three spindly legs.

"Who first?" Prosper said. "Who's the first man to step foot on Planet Elpis?"

"I vote for Launce," I said, holding my hand up. "He gave us wings to get here."

"But you freed us from the pilot module," Launce said.

"That made me first to breathe the air after sucking in y'all's stank."

The rest of the guys voted for Launce, and we followed,

oldest to youngest: Cricket, Bel, Sal, Prosper, Degory, Randall, and me. We climbed down the hatch into the vestibule, and from there we opened the vestibule door onto our new world.

"It's slippery, be careful," Launce said once he had stepped out.

Prosper kissed the ground. Degory found a wall to embrace. I rubbed a seam of the sparkling blue stone.

"That's lapis lazuli," Bel said and caressed the seam. "Do you realize how much of it we've seen on our way in?" He put his forehead to the wall. "More than there exists on all of Earth. This is a special place."

"It's our home now," Sal said. He slapped the rock.

"Lapis Elpis," Randall said and repeated it a few times with violent glee.

"Lapis Elpis is right," Sal said. "That's the name of this place."

"Hope Stone," Bel said. "That's what those words mean."

"Hope Stone," Prosper echoed. "Lapis Elpis." He bellowed the name into the canyon, and the walls echoed it back several times. "The first word this rock has heard has been its own name, and she spoke it back to us. I feel the joy of the Lord rushing through me." He howled.

We all howled like wolves and heard our voices multiply into a symphony of salvation.

"We're safe," I said. "We made it."

Launce made me see him glance at the twenty-five-hundred-foot vertical drop below us. He then looked up at the where the broken rock disappeared into the cloud line, another eight thousand feet above.

"Okay, it's cold," Randall said, and he went back into the can.

"It is slippery, and next to such a precipice," Cricket said, and he also went back into the module.

Sal slapped the rock again and followed. So did the rest of us.

Launce was not happy with our hanging out, literally, on the edge of the rock and asked us not to move around too much inside the can so we would not slip off the edge with no power to thrust gently back to the water below. Neither could we put up the tent, which would act like a sail for the wind to push. He would not even let Sal pass the whisky bottle around in case we became rowdy.

"One swift wind," Launce kept saying, a mantra of anxiety.

"One. Swift. Wind," the guys repeated in imitation of the warehouse warden.

"That's what we should call this tuna can," I said. "One Swift Wind."

Launce said, "You call it whatever you want when you're on duty."

"It's almost time for our daytime sleep," Cricket said. "I'm feeling it already. It's been a full day."

He lay down on top of the module with no tent in place.

"You've got a seat to strap into," Launce said, from below.

"I won't squirm around," Cricket said. "I'm not like Shelton, who tosses and turns like a little toddler."

"I resent that," I said half-jokingly.

"You're going to burn," Bel said, from his cell.

"You sound like my preacher back home," Cricket said.

"I mean under the sun. You can't sleep eight hours out here without burning up, not even under this cloud cover."

Cricket huffed. "It is still cold." He went into his cell.

"It's just for today, man," Launce said. "Of course we're gonna have days that break our rhythm."

"Better that than break our bones," I said if only to get back at Cricket.

"Amen," Prosper said. "I'm strapping in for the night. And by 'night,' I mean noon on Lapis Elpis."

It was an hour before noon, seventeen hours into the day. Bel and I played chess on the computer, but I would forget to move, staring out the window at Lapis Elpis. We did not finish the game before I fell asleep.

***

I woke up, four fitful hours later, to the can ascending. The batteries had recharged. Launce had not slept at all. The canyon dissolved into a white haze, and we were in the clouds. A few minutes later, blinding white sunlight poured into my cell just like it had when we had first emerged from the ocean. This time, though, we hovered above an endless sea of clouds. We had blue sky above.

"Not quite blue, though, is it?" Sal said, yawning. "More like turquoise."

"It ain't Earth, that's for sure," I said.

"That's not the weirdest thing," Bel said. "Take a look at our moon."

Launce spun the module so we could each catch a glimpse through our windows, but we had to crane our necks. I climbed up my hatch to see from above.

The sun, a few hours past noon, had put a crescent of

light on the moon. Through the turquoise sky, I could barely make out broad bands of blue, green, and gold.

"That's no moon," Prosper said, poking his head out, too.

"That's the planet we were supposed to be on," I said. "Then where the hell are we?"

Prosper looked at me. "We're the moon. Of that planet. Planet Doris."

"Of course we are," Bel said. "We got slingshot away from Doris and into this moon. With the clouds above us, we couldn't see that planet for what it was. We just assumed we were on our own planet, with its own moon. Very Earth-centric of us."

"Man, we don't even get our own planet?" Launce said, coming up.

"Who's flying?" I said.

"I say this is the planet, Lapis Elpis," Sal said. "Doris can play the moon for us."

"We're very clearly on the smaller body," Bel said. "Doris is almost the size of Jupiter."

"So, what?" Sal said. "It's acting like our moon, hanging out in the sky."

"Now you sound like Cricket, talking about east becoming west," Bel said.

"Who's flying?" I said again.

"It's on autopilot," Launce said. "Weren't we promised a planet?"

"We weren't promised anything," Bel said. "We have autopilot?"

"We sure do. I came into this fully expecting my own planet. Now I'm just a moon."

"Better this habitable moon than death on that planet," Bel said.

"I agree," Cricket said.

Degory and Randall had come up, too.

"I just feel second class is all," Launce said. "But what's new."

He went back into his cell and thrust the can forward, into the continent.

I endured the biting wind and was glad I did. In just a few minutes, I saw the clouds lapping up against a gently sloping shore of bare gray rock. I called everyone back up.

"Here is the place," Prosper said.

We landed. This time, there was room enough for all of us to do cartwheels, bare rock as far as we could see.

"This is us," Sal said, from behind me. He was looking east, toward the endless upward slope. I was looking west, with a sea of clouds at my feet.

"It was no mountain range at all," Launce said, "what we saw by the sea. It was the edge of this plateau. A mesa, if you will."

"I'll see your mesa and raise you a continent," Bel said. "I bet we're seeing the very beginnings of this place. Hot, shallow ocean, one landmass emerging from the tidal pull of the planet above us."

I stood looking north at the line of clouds lapping against the bare gray rock.

"I hope it's not all like this," Cricket said. "We do have

to plant our seed somewhere. Hidden Rats are only going to feed us so long."

"The man is right about that," Prosper said. "It can't all be like this."

"That's what we're here for, right?" Sal said. "To fertilize this place? We eat our rations, then we eat each other, then we fall over and die."

"Hold on now," Prosper said. "Should it come to that moment, I will be the first to let you men feed on me. But we're not there yet. Praise God, we're alive. We're standing our own two feet on Lapis Elpis, a moon to ourselves, as far as we know. And we know very little. What we're seeing is all we've seen so far. Maybe it's a continent, maybe it's an island. We've got time, and we've got hope, and I don't know of a more powerful mixture than that for a man to do his good work."

"Amen, brother," Launce said and lay down.

***

A few very quiet minutes later, I heard new sounds coming from the module. A bag hit the ground. I turned and saw Degory, in full winter clothes, carrying all his gear: backpack, pup tent, sleeping bag. I stuck out my chin. He nodded and walked away.

"Degory," I said.

The other guys watched him pass through. Prosper studied him. Sal shrugged. When Degory reached the top of a low rise, a few hundred yards away toward the northeast, he turned, saluted, and continued on his way.

"Let him," Sal said.

Prosper nodded.

"I thought you'd be all about keeping us together," I said to Prosper.

"It depends, I suppose," Prosper said. "But that's a bad hombre. *Lupo loco.*"

"Whatever, we're all bad hombres," I said.

The guys looked at me.

"Some of us are badder than others, some of us not so bad at all," Sal said. "You pay attention long enough, you'll find most groups self-selecting. He knew once we landed he wasn't gonna be welcome too long."

"'*Volcán, fuego de este hogar,*'" Bel said. "That's what he typed before he left. '*La huelo.*' I smell it. But *volcán*, *fuego*, and *hogar* are all masculine nouns."

"Her, man," Launce said. "I smell *her*. His mother, what's her name."

"Chantico," I said. "I don't smell a volcano or a fire."

"None of us do," Sal said. "But he does, or thinks he does, and that's the point. You know how the guys get jumped in to that gang? They're not beat up, like normal. Hot coals. He takes off his shirt, and you're going to see their brand on his chest and back. The tattoos all start from there."

"Maybe he's gonna jump in a volcano, take one for the team," I said.

"That's one way of looking at it," Sal said.

"Well, I'm relieved," Cricket said. "I was worried he was going to eat me in my sleep."

Sal rolled his eyes and whispered, "You wish."

"He took all his rations," Bel said, from the module. "Left the walls of his cell a mess, all kinds of weird carvings."

"We can use it for storage," Launce said. He had not fallen asleep before Degory had left. "Another thing good ol' Doris didn't think to give us. Extra water, et cetera."

"We should find a place with water," Prosper said.

"Yeah," Launce said. "Need be, we can always dip down into the gorge again. But that's a hop in itself, half a day's battery." He rubbed his eyes. "Speaking of battery, mine's running a bit low. Perhaps one of you all can take us up somewhere, let me get some shut-eye."

"I'll do it," I said. "You guys just tell me where to go."

We crossed north of the fjord we had followed inland, and I thought I heard more than one sigh of relief that there was now a hard barrier between us and Degory. I had no idea what the other guys had been thinking or saying about him. Degory and I had played chess together a few times. I was sure they understood what Degory was better than I ever could. That mattered on this lifeless rock.

We flew for a couple hours. Along the way, the gray rock rolled below us, smooth and featureless. We landed near a low cliff face to recharge. The cliff would act as a windbreak. I was glad the other guys were still around to think about things like windbreaks.

After helping put up the dome tent and lying down for a short sleep, I felt much more at ease, so much so I forgot to put my knife under my pillow. These guys were not all the same, and they were looking out for each other, me included. If Degory was a bad hombre, he had been the bad apple of the group. Now that he was gone, I wondered who among us was the craziest.

14

I woke up from the deepest part of sleep, sometime later, to find Cricket's face hovering over me in the dome tent. He was surrounded by golden light, and his smile, which I usually found to be drawn by someone who had heard of a smile but never seen one, seemed genuine now. When the rational part of my brain discovered that my eyes were open, I jumped and reached for my knife, which was not there.

"It's alright, it's alright," Cricket said. "We just thought you'd want to see our first sunset."

"Sunset? Sunset? Are y'all hard-ass convicts or what?" I said and rubbed my face.

Outside, the cloud layer had risen to the side of our cliff. I could hardly see the rock on which the module was resting. The western horizon was already three shades of orange, and soon the white clouds absorbed all the gold our setting sun had to give.

"Damn, alright," I said. "Beautiful."

"She approves," Prosper said. "Lapis Elpis has rolled out the golden carpet for us."

"This is something to behold," Launce said.

Randall was sitting down where the clouds covered everything but his head. I joined him until the clouds blocked my vision.

"Take a look at Planet Doris, too," Cricket said.

To the east, the planet we were orbiting was half-lit, showing off its bands of blue, green, and gold.

"We've got to find a real name for it," Bel said. "Something good but not too good. I'm with Launce here, somewhat ambivalent about having to orbit another planet."

"The old ball and chain," Sal said. "What's that in Greek? Gyro Spiro? Randall likes it. Lapis Elpis, meet Gyro Spiro."

"I think they met a long time ago," Bel said. "Or we'd be in a lot of trouble."

"What's that supposed to mean?" I said.

"It means that if we're not in a stable orbit around," he huffed, "Gyro Spiro, or whatever we actually end up calling it, who knows what our next sunset looks like."

"Well, so far, so good," Launce said.

The clouds were up to our shoulders now, or mine anyway, standing up.

"Do we have to hover up to a higher level or what?" I said. "I mean, are these clouds going to suffocate us?"

"Suffocate us?" Launce said, laughing. "You never been in fog? That's all clouds are when they're on the ground."

"Still, our equipment and all."

"We began life on this planet in the ocean. The Ardeen'll be just fine, won't you, girl?" He slapped the side of the module.

Cricket said, "Yeah, well, it's going to be grotesquely humid in the tent. And before you talk about flying in the dark, we can see the terrain by laser light. The lidar will tell us where to land."

The sun had just fallen below the horizon, leaving us in twilight.

"The man's got a point," Sal said. "I'm getting soaked already. The rock keeps going up from here."

It took going ten miles deeper inland to land a thousand feet higher. The lidar map showed us on a flat slab of rock. The light from the Jolly Green Giant, as Sal was now calling the planet above us, made shadows that showed the rock full of ruts in which we could twist our ankles. Launce forbade us from walking out there in the dark.

"Not the Jolly Green Giant," Cricket said, right when I was about to fall asleep again, under the dome tent. "You all remember the story of Jack and the beanstalk from when you were kids."

No one answered. I had a vague recollection.

"Yeah, come on. That's us, Jack. We built a beanstalk from Earth to skies full of gold, and now we've found the giant. We've simply got to make away with this world's goods and send the signal to dear old Doris before he finds us. What was his name?"

"Blunderbore," Bel said.

"No, it wasn't that," Cricket said.

"Trust me," Bel said. "You're talking to a *Jeopardy!* winner here."

A memory flashed before me of my mother reading to me. I loved her, but she had always reeked of cigarette smoke. A whiff of that nicotine smell came to me, and I saw the name clearly written on the page of the book.

"Gogmagog," I said.

"That's it," Cricket said.

"In some variants of the story," Bel said.

"Gogmagog, perfect," Sal said. "That's what we call the green giant above us. Lapis Elpis, meet Gogmagog."

"Very biblical," Prosper said. "Gog and Magog are defeated by Christ at the end of time. Book of Revelations, Chapter Twenty."

No one spoke while we gazed upward at Gogmagog, the planet around which we orbited, our monstrous master. My eyes began to droop.

Bel said, "I propose we now take about six to eight hours, in silence, to think about how we're going to build a beanstalk back to Earth. When you figure it out, I will be the first one to tell Dr. Huntsman. In the meantime, I will be sleeping."

"Look who's calling the shots around here now," Cricket said.

"I'm not calling any shots. Just trying to keep us on schedule. I need my beauty sleep. And by the look of things, so do you."

"Of course you want to be the first one to tell Dr. Huntsman," Cricket said. "You were the teacher's pet back there, the way she smiled when you got in her face."

I had not been the only one to notice.

"Y'all sound like little kids. Especially you, old man," Launce said.

"Old man?" Cricket said. "I'll show you old man."

"Come on now," Prosper said. "Let's call it a night. Bel here is right. Time to get back on schedule."

Randall farted then laughed about it.

"That's making the beans talk," Sal said. "We've got our own gas giant here."

We all laughed and, eventually, fell asleep.

15

When I woke up again, the dome tent was glowing from outside. It was just me, Bel, and Randall lying down. A couple of guys were outside, talking low. I went down. Gogmagog was fully lit, casting the rocky world around us in blue-green light. I could see by that light where it was safe enough to walk and met up with Launce, Sal, and Cricket.

"Where's Prosper?" I said.

"Planting the first garden," Sal said. "Dumped half his litter box into some grooves in the rock. He's been studying the seed packets to see which goes best for this, uh, what'd he call it?"

"Climatic zone," Launce said.

"He settled on Arctic Taiga," Sal said, "based on how cold it is. Says we'll get pine trees coming out of his poop in no time."

"That's the kind of science your average death-row inmate will give you," I said.

"Oh, no, he's a lifer, remember," Sal said, tapping the side of his head. "That makes him smarter. Smart enough not to get caught."

"Smart enough not to do any worse than he did," Launce said.

"Not smart enough to think about water," I said. "There's no water up here, and I haven't seen any clouds above us."

"Take a look," Launce said, and he pointed to where we had come from.

The clouds had come up quickly during the night, from the place we had labeled Sunset Cliffs.

"We're getting chased up a mountain by those clouds," Launce said. "A little higher, and we won't have much air to breathe."

"We just let the clouds pass," Sal said. "So maybe we've got to spend a night or two in the can to keep from getting wet. Cricket won't mind, will you?"

Cricket was staring upward, at the many stars still visible through Gogmagog's glow.

Sal saw that Cricket was awe-stricken, bounced his eyebrows at me, and kicked a small rock. He bent over, picked up another rock, bounced it in his hand, and put it in his pocket.

"Make sure you label it correctly in your collection," I said. "What's our name for this place, anyway? Prosper's Pine Grove?"

"Just Pine Grove would be fine," Prosper said, joining us. "The seeds I've planted will one day fill this whole world. You know what? Call it Pine Groove. Yeah, that's it. Pine Groove."

I looked around. "Now what do we do?"

"Do you fellows see any constellations you recognize?"

Cricket said. "We could figure out where in the universe we are."

I looked up. "I know the constellations. You get to see a lot of north, on your own. And I don't recognize anything. Not the Pleiades, nothing."

"But then again," Prosper said, "Gogmagog is burning bright, and we didn't see the stars on the other side of Lapis Elpis. So, let's not count ourselves out just yet."

From the module came the sound of clanging metal. Bel came out with his litter box. "I like our odds up here, between the grooves and the clouds. Plus, it's getting a little rank inside. If the clouds are rising, that means air pressure with it. Prosper planted taiga. I'm going to do a tundra-highlands mix. Not too much. We've got a lot of ground to cover. Get some gloves if you're going to fill your own groove, too. Keep the unused kitty litter."

I looked at Launce, Sal, and Cricket. "Are we actually doing this?"

"Nothing better to do right now," Sal said, and he went into the module. Once inside, he said, "Come on, Randall, time to get to work."

Randall groaned.

Under the swamp-gas light of Gogmagog, the seven of us planted our first garden into the narrow grooves of rock. Bel had figured out earlier that we were located about twenty degrees south latitude on a moon not much smaller than Earth, so I picked a seed packet based on what grew in New York, figuring that if the clouds were coming up, the air would get warmer. I wanted oaks but also knew how quickly birch trees grew, having seen so many of them take over whole abandoned properties.

"How do you know this place is smaller than Earth?" I said.

"Can't you feel it?" Bel said. "Less gravity. I'm practically bouncing."

"You've probably just lost weight over the past month, eating nothing but Hidden Rats," I said. "Whereas I have not."

"You've got no weight to lose," Sal said.

"True, and therefore, I can be the…what do you call that in science, the thing that doesn't change?"

"The placenta," Launce said.

"You mean placebo," Bel said. "There's nothing resembling a placenta around here. And Shelton means the control group. The group unaffected by the change. We'd have to do the old stick-and-shadow trick to measure the circumference of Lapis Elpis, the way the Greeks did it. The computer can't tell us. Not yet. It just feels like there's less gravity."

"You and your Greeks," Sal said. He slapped his belly. "But I concur. I've got a new spring in my step, too. How about you, Randall? Feeling any lighter? Randall?"

"I do now," Randall said, from the other side of the module. "Can we put toilet paper in the garden?"

I finished planting my grass and trees and looked up at Gogmagog. A dark dot I had not seen before was slowly crossing it. "What's that? A storm, like on Jupiter? Maybe the actual portal? With less gravity, we could get our beanstalks reaching up there in no time."

"What are you even talking about?" Bel said, squinting his eyes.

"I see it," Launce said. "Looks like a mole."

"There's a bit of sand in these cracks," Prosper said. "That's good, right? It's not all just bare rock?"

"That is good," Cricket said. "A bit of sand in the soil will give it air, let it drain. You see any more sand around?"

"I do," Randall said. "All around here."

"Well, let's come on, then," Cricket said. "Load up."

I sighed. "Isn't the cat litter good enough?"

"Not when there's something better," Cricket said. "Plus, the stuff they gave us is fibrous, corncobs and paper, designed to clump together before dissolving. Trust me. This is my life's work."

I scoured the nearby grooves for a few pockets full of sand and returned to my area.

Sal sided up to me and spoke quietly. "Like he's some kind of gardener. He mows lawns for a living. You've seen his paperwork. Knows more about cutting than planting, I would say."

"You know, I've not actually read y'all's paperwork. I'm doing what Prosper said. Besides, he said he didn't do it."

"Yeah, right. None of us did it."

"Whatever. Either way, maybe the man's right. We get a fresh start here."

"Or a fresh finish. Keep that knife under your pillow. Like Launce said, some of us are badder than others. You're hard but not hard enough, smart but not smart enough."

"I think that's us," Prosper said. "That's our shadow on Gogmagog's belly. Right? With the sun behind us like this?"

"Huh," Bel said.

"Well, I'll be," Launce said. "Everyone wave at ourselves."

I waved, the only one who did so, and quickly tucked my hand back into my pocket.

"They eclipse us, we eclipse them," Cricket said.

"Who's them?" Prosper said.

"You know what I mean," Cricket said. "Our shadow selves, on the surface of Gogmagog."

"The ghosts trapped in Gogmagog," Randall said. "The souls we have to free."

"That's not what I meant," Cricket said.

Randall stared at Cricket for a few seconds then turned away.

Cricket made to say something else, but Prosper put up his hands and shook his head. When he was sure Randall could not hear, Cricket said, "What possessed him to say that?"

"Possessed is right," Prosper said. "So don't touch it."

I looked at Sal, who shrugged and said, "What do I know? I just met the guy, too."

After a quiet minute, Launce said, "We've got enough battery for another hop. But how about we stay, let the clouds pass, check on our work when the sun rises again? Just a full night of rest."

"This night lasts another full Earth day," I said. Where I was eager to go next, I did not know. "What do we do, just hang around in the dark?"

"We haven't taken a proper sabbath," Prosper said.

"Sure, that, too," Launce said.

"Launce makes a good point," Bel said. "It would be good to watch what this world does with our planting."

The clouds had come up to the module by the time we finished taking down the tent. As much as I had wanted to walk around and stretch my legs on Lapis Elpis, sitting in my comfortable chair in the dry heat the can fed into my cell was a relief from the damp chill of the rising fog. Bel and I played chess.

"Doing a little research on the computer, I'm somewhat glad there aren't lifeforms here already," Bel said.

"That we know about," Prosper said.

"That we know about," Bel said. "But I'm talking about right-handed sugar."

"Of course, you are," Launce said.

"I once knew a girl named Right Hand Sugar," Sal said.

"Of course you did," Launce said.

"I'm talking about chirality," Bel said.

"Watch your language," Sal said. "She was a good girl, in the end."

"Every sugar on Earth is right-handed," Bel said. "That's what I mean by chirality."

"My girl was left-handed," Launce said.

"Do you guys want to learn something or not?"

"No, not really," Sal said.

"Well, you're going to anyway. All glucose is built a certain way. It goes right or it goes left. Up here, on a different planet—"

"Moon," I said.

"Not now, Shelton. Make your move. And watch your queen."

Bel was right. He could see I was about to take with my knight, exposing my queen to attack.

"Up here, as I was saying, we could have had vegetation and creatures made for left-handed sugar. L-Glucose. Impossible for us to digest. It would have been sugar sugar everywhere, and not a grain to eat."

"Sounds like when I'm walking with my girl downtown," Launce said.

"Y'all are too much," I said.

Bel checkmated me. He had been the one talking during our whole game, and he checkmated me, who had said next to nothing. But he had got the guys going, and that had distracted me.

"As it is, we'll have to see if our plants can even take in nutrients here," Bel said.

"That would take weeks," Cricket said, joining the conversation. "I say we explore and come back."

"In the morning," Launce said. "We check our work, first."

"I'm already tired of sitting here," Cricket said.

"Me, too," Randall said. "I'm going back outside."

"You're gonna get your clothes soaked," Sal said.

"Not if I'm naked," Randall said.

"God help us," I said.

"Indeed," Prosper said.

Randall was not kidding. He went outside, naked, and stomped around the module like a monster, glowing green in the light and declaring himself the incarnation of Gogmagog. After a few minutes, he came back in and said, "Okay, it's cold."

"I hope someone's writing all this down, for posterity's sake," Prosper said.

No one answered.

"A captain's log, anything. Bel, you're the most eloquent among us," Prosper said.

"I've been keeping my own journal," Cricket said. "Aren't the rest of you?"

Again, no one answered, so I said, "I do sketches."

"Have you sketched us?" Cricket said.

"Little bit, here and there."

"Show us."

I held up my sketchpad to the computer camera.

"Nice," Launce said. "Who's the lady? Is that Mireille?"

"This one's actually my mom."

"Nice," Launce said. "She see you off?"

"I saw her off," I said. "Lung cancer. Five years ago. We had nothing, you know, growing up. She tried, but we had nothing. I finished high school and figured who needs years of trade school when a whole world is up there, ready to be taken? That's when I got into collecting, three years ago. Little did I know."

"Sorry about your mom," Launce said, and the other guys echoed his condolences.

"Nah, it's just that she's actually the hardest to draw. Her smile. I never get her smile right."

"That's your mother, man," Launce said. "She's always going to be more angel to you than human."

I almost answered Launce but kept my mother's past to myself.

Bel pinged me for a sidebar conversation.

"Can I ask you a question, with no disrespect involved?" Bel said.

"You gonna ask about my mother some more?"

"What I mean is, trying to get her smile right, maybe there are some things to consider."

"Bel, you gotta just talk straight with me."

"Was she smart?"

I pulled my head back. "What's that got to do with it?"

"You said you guys struggled. Did she work?"

I sighed. "She couldn't keep a job for more than a year, anywhere. I see where you're going with this. Yeah, I actually worked at the same grocery store with her for a few months, before she got sick. Probably the best job she ever had, at the checkout. I could see there what I couldn't see at home. Some people can think through their situations, you know, see what's in front of them. My mom, she got easily confused. Sweet as hell, you know. Some people took advantage of that. That smile, yeah, it was a stupid smile. Sweet, but stupid."

"That's all I mean," Bel said. "Intelligence plays a lot more than some people realize, even on a smile. You take guys in prison. Some are there because they're stupid, can't make it the normal way, just start trying to take what they can. Other guys are there because they're smarter than everyone around them and make the world a game, finding new ways to take advantage. The rest of us, we just had a stupid moment or two. I'm smart but not a genius. I just appreciate knowledge. You're a curator of things from the old world, I'm a curator of its knowledge. But I know enough now to recognize that of all the qualities that draw people together, intelligence is a big factor. You'll get tired of living with someone stupider or smarter than yourself.

"My wife was smart, a real genius, and that was what led to our problems in the end. She couldn't put up with me anymore, and I mirrored that back at her. Long story short, see if you can draw your mom, as sweet as she was, but knowing she was not smart. Love her for what she was, human not angel."

"Look, I know how human she was. She was a prostitute," I said. "Up until she had me. She said I saved her life. She never said how, but when I got older and learned the world a bit, figured out who her old friends were, the old guys who would lend her money, I knew. She never knew I knew. So that's us, Bel. That's me and my mom, the story of our sad, stupid life. She died when I was sixteen. I worked, saved up enough money to buy a truck, and I went up north. Two years on my own, I've killed a cop for no good reason—well, that's a story for another time, as they say. And now I'm stuffing my shit into the cracks of some alien moon, waiting to see what grows. If that ain't stupid, I don't know what is. I'll draw my mom with angel wings, smiling down from heaven on her stupid-ass son, waiting for him to finally get himself killed so he can see her again."

"Not so fast, Shelton. I've got a feeling we're on to something here, something more than meets the eye. But that's a story for another time, as they say. A theory in development."

"Three hours," Prosper said on the intercom. "That's how long it took for our shadow to cross Gogmagog."

"Good," Bel said to everyone. "Tomorrow night, let's take a more accurate reading. I'm working on an idea here."

16

The rest of the thirty-six hour night passed slowly. The clouds had risen past us by the time our second sleep came around, so we put up the dome tent again and stretched out. Doing nothing in one place for almost twenty hours is no good for getting sleep, though, and I spent some time outside, looking up at the stars, trying to find any shared constellations with Earth. There were none.

When the sun finally rose, our gardens looked a lot like they had under the light of Gogmagog, thin streaks of brown mud stuffed into the crevices of dark gray rock. The fog had moistened them.

"That's it?" I said. "We stayed here all night for this?"

"You in a hurry to get somewhere else?" Launce said.

I shrugged.

"Now that the clouds are above us and land is below us, like a planet should be, we can take our time, do things right," Launce said. "Proper procedure and protocol, if you will."

"I agree," Bel said. "I'm glad we stayed. The only way to win this thing is to use time to our advantage."

"Win this thing?" I said. "We've already lost. I thought that's why we're here."

"Come on now," Prosper said. "We've already won. We're the first human beings on this moon-planet, and we're giving it life. This little garden says so. This is our flag of victory. Come on, Keyes. Time is ours now."

I saluted my streak of mud in the ground.

"That's the spirit," Launce said. "Now let's go find us a lake or a river."

We followed a low ridge northward for nearly a whole day, thirty-four hours. With the clouds a few hundred feet above us and rising, we had great visibility. The rock we had passed in the canyon, light gray with streaks of lapis lazuli, gave way to the dark gray granite and patches of black volcanic sand. Otherwise, very little changed in the landscape.

Near sunset, we finally stopped at one of those fields of black volcanic sand, which Cricket told us made nutritious soil. We were shoveling it into the remaining body bags for planting elsewhere. Bel and Launce started arguing about something.

"What all of us have been trying to say is that the whole day, night included, is getting shorter," Launce said. "Take this sunset about to happen. I've got it a full thirty minutes less than when we first landed."

"I'm saying it has to do with our changing latitude," Bel said, as he shoveled a load into a bag.

"You're talking to a Navy man here. And a Navy man knows time."

"Then we chalk it up to relativity," Bel said. "Gogmagog has a lot of gravity. Time goes faster for us the closer we get."

"You're no scientist," Launce said.

"No, I'm not," Bel said. "And neither are you."

"Whoa whoa whoa," Launce said in my direction.

"Come on now," Prosper said. "Cut out the fighting."

"No, I'm talking to Keyes here. Stop shoveling. Hold on, there." He bent over and sifted through the sand I had shoveled into the bag we shared. He picked up a clear rock between his fingers and held it to the low sun. "My friends, I think that this here is a diamond."

Sal thrust his hand out. "I'll tell you for sure." He huffed on it, held it to the light, and tried to read the fine print on a rations wrapper through it. "Yes, it is. About eight carats. Launce, this is about a quarter of a million dollars you just found."

The seven of us stood around Launce's open hand, staring at the diamond.

Launce turned away. "Just laying here in the sand?"

Randall walked twenty feet away, bent over, and picked up another smaller diamond. "Just lying here in the sand."

I put the shovel down. The low sun made the volcanic sand glisten, but it also sparkled in a few places. The seven of us combed the field.

"Found one," Bel said.

"Damn," I said, and I kept looking.

Launce started singing:

Gonna jump down, turn around
Pick a bale of cotton
Gonna jump down, turn around
Pick a bale a day

Oh lordy, pick a bale of cotton
Oh lordy, pick a bale a day

We all picked up the lyrics and sang along. One by one, the other guys found diamonds, sometimes two or three each. I found nothing, but I kept singing to keep my spirits up:

Gonna jump down, turn around
Pick a bale of cotton
Gonna jump down, turn around
Pick a bale a day
Oh lordy, pick a bale of cotton
Oh lordy, pick a bale a day

Suddenly, Prosper's deep voice came booming, and he sang:

Dat nigger from Shiloh
Kin pick a bale o' cotton
Dat nigger from Shiloh
Kin pick a bale a day

"What the hell, Prosper?" Launce said. "Those aren't the words."

"They used to be," Prosper said.

"What exactly is your point, then?" Launce said.

"If you're going to sing a slave song, sing it right. Not your white-washed version."

"Oh, I get it," Launce said. "The one Black guy on our trip has finally got to say his piece."

"What about me?" I said.

"You said it yourself, Keyes. Your mom's white. And you're not the one trying to give us all a lesson in slave songs like you got a bone to pick about something else."

"That is not the lesson," Prosper said. "Have we had any trouble so far? Did you see me reluctant at all to join you guys in Module Nine? No, brother. I saw promise. And that's what I want to talk about now. Look at this."

He pulled out his pockets to show he had not tried to collect any diamonds.

"So, what?" Launce said.

"So, if you're working like slaves, sing like slaves really used to."

"Who's working like slaves around here?" Launce said.

"Where are you gonna sell those diamonds?" Prosper said. "You all haven't learned yet. You've brought earthly greed to Lapis Elpis. We are still slaves in the field. Still slaves to Earth's economy, Earth's values."

"Hold on there, Prosper," Sal said. "Like you, yourself, keep saying, we don't know where all this ends. We don't know we won't get back to Earth. We've walked only a hundred feet across this valley and put a million dollars in our pockets. You try to see all things in light of God, well, here it is. He's providing for us right now, giving us something to trade, perhaps."

"I think he's right, Prosper," Launce said. "Take it as a sign of God's favor. Even if it's worth nothing in the economy of Gogmagog and its moons, wear it like a jewel. Just because you've got to bend your back once in a while to earn a dollar doesn't make you a slave."

Prosper put his pockets back in and held his hands there. He smacked his lips, pulled out his hands, bent over, and started brushing through the sand. He picked up a small diamond, showed it to Sal and Launce, and put it in his breast pocket. "To the glory of God."

I looked up to a turquoise sky turning orange and bent over. The sun began to set, and a deep charcoal shadow came over the field, cast by a hill behind us. There were no diamonds at my feet, no matter how far down I dug.

Cricket approached me, holding out a diamond. "Here, Shelton. Don't leave empty-handed."

I put up my palms and said, "I won't, trust me. Just let me find my own."

"Suit yourself."

I looked ahead, where the shadow had not yet fallen on the field. I could run down there and search with the remaining sunlight, but some truth in what Prosper and Launce had said stopped me. I did not particularly believe in God, but I knew how to find and collect things, and my best work was always done by myself, with patience. What was more, I knew how to work, and the first and last time anyone had given me anything, like Cricket had tried to do just now, had led to my killing a cop.

17

The next morning, after a couple of night hops to places we called Not Fresh Water and God's Belly Button, I woke up in a place we had not yet named. The air had been growing warmer with each hop northward, toward the equator, and I sat outside, eating a bowl of very mushy rations, waiting for the sun to rise. Some guys, like Randall, gnawed on the raw wafers. Other guys, like Cricket, boasted about the perfect consistency they had achieved through strict ratios of water and time. I liked eating Hidden Rats like oatmeal. I was not ready to lose a tooth in a world without dentists or compete with Cricket about anything.

We followed the land northward, along a valley, figuring it would eventually fill with a river. We were running low on water. Lapis Elpis paid us a happy surprise, though, when we came across a dormant volcano, whose crater was filled with fresh water.

"Tastes fine to me," Randall said. He scooped up a handful before any of us could warn him not to, before Bel could test it with a kit we had. "Tastes sweet."

While I was watching Bel test the ph levels, Cricket passed behind him, into the lake, completely naked.

"Yo, that's not the idea," I said. "We're not gonna drink where we pee."

Cricket ignored me and did backstrokes.

Randall, Sal, Prosper, and Launce all jumped in to bathe, wearing at least their underwear.

Bel rolled his eyes and shrugged. "The water's fine." He sniffed his armpit. "Might as well."

The water was perfectly clear and very cold. When I finished bathing, I came back to shore to find Cricket lying naked on the rock.

"That's not the right idea, either," I said, turning to Sal.

"He's fishing," Sal said.

"Well, tell him to cast his rod in another direction."

Cricket, overhearing this, smiled and said, "Relax, Shelton. We're all men here."

Sal said to him, "What that means to us and what that means to you are two different things."

Randall stood over Cricket with his hands on his hips.

"Having a good look?" Cricket said. When Randall did not move, he said, "Alright," and put his jumpsuit back on. "But all I meant was, who else is around? It's just us."

"I think that's the point," Prosper said. "It's just us, and we've still got a lot of living to do together, in pretty tight quarters. As big as this world is, we're only going to live by sticking together and making each other's lives as easy as possible. We're doing alright, so far."

The rim of the dead volcano seemed an ideal place to sow more seeds, but we had very little fertilizer left over. As a sign of unity, Bel suggested we mix what we had with some fine rock chips we made with our picks. We planted a few kinds of grass and trees, refilled the water tank in the module, and moved on from the place we called Clearwater Crater.

As we continued north, we noticed a pattern to the land. Long, low ridges ran parallel to the shoreline a few miles to our west, and these were made of smaller parallel ridges, from a few feet to a few hundred feet wide.

It made sense to all of us, then, when Launce suggested we turn northeast, across these ridges, and see if a change in landscape brought us to streams, rivers, and lakes. In a five-hour hop, we could cover two hundred miles, and this would take us pretty deep into the continent. The system of parallel ridges continued for all of that distance, but to our surprise, it fell lower and lower. The eleven-thousand-foot escarpment we had first encountered at the sea's edge was the highest the land around here had risen. It sunk, from there, toward to the northeast, as if the whole continent were in the ribbed, circular shape of a stereo speaker, broken only by the occasional chasm like the one through which we had made landfall.

Ideally, we could travel up to twelve hundred miles a day, but hover tech, just like wheeled cars, spent more energy going over hills, and we stopped somewhat frequently to look at the changing landscape. We gave names to every place we stopped—Little Green Snake Hill, Vanishing Creek, Sal's Dance—and many places we passed, like Sulfur Spring, Flock of Sheep (which Bel explained were a geologic feature called drumlins), and Warden's Boot. The ground was softer the lower we went, proof that wind and water had been working the land longer than it had seemed when we'd first arrived. Bel said cryptically that this worked against his theory, which he had not yet explained.

We went on for nights and days like this, Lapis Elpis time, trying as best we could to match our Earthling bodies to the changing day. Launce kept mentioning that the days were growing shorter, and Bel could no longer argue against him.

One morning, the sun rose in a sliver of turquoise between distant rugged mountains and a low-lying blanket of clouds. It was shaped like an upside-down pear. The other guys noticed it, too. Bel attributed it to atmospheric gas, the same thing that made the stars twinkle.

The pear-sun held our attention until it passed behind the clouds, when I heard Sal whistle behind me. He had walked about a hundred yards away and was looking at a large blue rock jutting from the adjoining gray. By the time I finished eating my breakfast and cleaning the bowl and spoon, the rest of the guys had joined him. They were stroking the smooth, sculpted edges of the rock like it was a car.

I approached and saw that it was lapis lazuli, the same stuff we had seen in seams when we had first made landfall. This piece was the size of a tank and was worn very smooth. Flecks of gold sparkled in the field of deep blue. I liked it as much as any of the guys—until I did not.

Before my brain could calm me down, some inner animal reacted to the shiny rock and trembled and raged inside me. I felt like I thought Randall always looked, like the slightest threat would be met with a fist or a knife. I had to test this thing against reality, to make sure it was not some emergence of a nightmare. I grabbed a pick and chipped away at it.

"What are you doing?" Sal said.

"He's still upset he didn't get a diamond the other day," Cricket said.

"That's not it," I said, and I held a large chip in my hand. It was smooth on one side and rough on the other. "I get it now. This whole place, this whole damn planet, is our judgment. This is mine."

"Now you're being cryptic," Bel said.

"Never mind," I said, and I threw the chip as far as I could.

"Come on now," Prosper said. "If this is a moment of truth, tell us. Don't carry this cross on your own."

I looked at the guys, none of whom, apart from Prosper, seemed particularly eager to hear what I had to say. "Y'all don't want my truth."

"Your truth?" Cricket said. "Tell us, young man, about your truth."

"Come on," Sal said. "Leave him alone. We've all got baggage. There's a reason he's here with us."

"He killed a cop," Randall said. "What's more to it? Huh, Keyes?"

I sighed. "You see, Prosper? They don't want my truth. Don't even want to think there is one."

"I just don't see how a rock is supposed to make you so upset," Cricket said. "Especially when this world is nothing but rocks. What's so special about this rock, Shelton? Or have you just had it with this world altogether?"

I leaned my foot on the rock. "Y'all want to hear it or not?"

"Tell us," Launce said. "Get it off your chest, if you want."

"Don't play him like that," Prosper said. "Don't make his truth feel like a burden to you all just by hearing it. We've all got things we're working through. No one's asking you others to tell the story behind your paperwork. Not yet, and maybe Lapis Elpis will make you tell your story, one way or another. Keyes and Randall here are the only ones to tell us in their own voice what they did to get here. Maybe we all read each other's paperwork, maybe not. But if the man wants to speak, let him speak."

"You see, that's just the first thing," I said. "I haven't read y'all's paperwork. I don't know what you done. You know me, and I respect the fact that you might not want to be known for what you did. So, I'll tell you, all of you, I'm not like you. I killed a cop, but I'm not a cop killer, if you get what I mean. Maybe you already know that, and that's why you don't want to hear it from someone not like yourselves."

"Hold on now, Keyes," Prosper said. "Let's do this right, without disrespecting nobody. You heard one of us say it before, that some of us are bad, some not so bad. We're all here for different reasons."

I leaned on my leg, still propped on the rock. No one spoke.

"It was a car," I said. "A Maserati. Dark blue metallic, just like this rock. Y'all want to hear it?"

"This sounds like a real story," Sal said. "Let's hear it."

"Alright, then. So, I'm collecting for a year or so, on my own. I've got a good system. There are no working gas stations north of I-80 anymore, so I find some roads to take my pickup north from there, as far as I can get on half a tank, plus the cans in the bed. From there, it's door to door by bicycle. Like a newsboy, only I'm taking what's old from the houses. I'm making money, especially on DVDs, small furniture, things I can carry. It's efficient, on my own.

"One day, I meet Mireille. Man, I've never seen a girl like this. She's confident, almost cocky, and I like that. She's got a small crew, two other guys. We start working together. They've got a big truck, with ramps and everything, so we can expand our reach by hitching my pickup to the truck. Soon, we're in neighborhoods, whole towns that haven't been touched in eighty years.

"We find a farmhouse one day, still intact, like the ghosts are taking care of it. I wake up in the morning, eat my breakfast just like we're doing now, and the barn is calling me. Like, I can practically hear it. I go in, and all I see is old straw, damp and gray and rotting. But this feeling won't let me leave, like something's calling me from under the straw. So, I start pulling it down. It becomes clear, pretty quick, that there's something underneath.

"Oh, my God, I cannot tell you gentlemen what it felt like that morning. By the time I got the straw off and saw the car under wraps, Mireille and the guys had come into the barn. Even before we got the cover off, I knew we were into something good. The car was up on blocks. The thing was wrapped underneath, too. Whoever covered this thing had prepared it for the long winter, like they knew the world was about to end, which it was.

"We were careful. We made sure not to put a scratch on

it as we pulled off the cover. And, oh, my God, there it was. A twenty-twenty-two Maserati GranTurismo in this color blue." I tapped the rock. "Perfect condition even after eighty years. All we had to do was fill the tires with air and push it onto the truck. Forget everything else, which we could come back for."

"I've never even heard of a Maserati," Sal said. "And I know things."

Bel made as if to say something, but he stopped.

"I tell you what, Sal," I said. "People have. People in St. Louis, people in Houston, and people in the Sahara. For an old-world car like that, with a minimum of restoration, they would pay top dollar. And they did. Eighty thousand dollars. Split four ways, for me, Mireille, and the other guys. I know for a fact that the people we sold it to, the New York people, turned it over for three times that to a guy in the Sahara, in Agadez Nouveau. I didn't mind, and I still don't, not about the money, not about splitting it. Mireille and the crew had the truck to get it out. All I did was find it.

"What I did mind, and still do, is everything that came after. That's what got me into New York, where I saw the lady with the world in her hands, inspiring me to get this tattoo. Mireille, man, she had been standoffish, you know, distant. But not that night. After we sold that car, it was drinks on top of the Empire State Building. After drinks, it was you know what."

Some of the guys smiled. I stood up straight.

"She wasn't my first, you know—that was one of my mom's old friends, after the funeral, feeling sorry or taking advantage of me, either way, it was what it was, but I didn't feel much different after—but after Mireille, I did. I felt like a man, finally. Proud. Like I could do anything. Standing literally and poetically on top of the world."

"And the only place from there is down," Bel said. "Sorry, Shelton. I didn't mean to interrupt."

"No, you nailed it," I said. "First thing was Mireille, not talking to me much the next day. Like she regretted it. So, I laid off. But the New York guys, they liked me. Said I had vision. Said if I wanted in, I was in. So, I thought I'd take the job, impress Mireille."

"Didn't work, did it?" Bel said.

"No."

"What attracted her about you was being on top of you, literally and poetically," Bel said.

"Now that you put it that way..." I said. "She liked having a bunch of guys hanging on her at all times, but at arm's length. Anyway, the New York guys send me with a shipment down to Tampa. As far as I know, it's collector goods. They pay my expenses and a hefty fee. Should've been my first clue. But I was a goddamned idiot, drunk on luck, and they knew that.

"I always carried a gun. You never know when a coyote is come up on you. So, I'm in this warehouse in Tampa, waiting for my connection. I hear footsteps. This is collector goods, in a secure location. I'm not worried about anyone stealing. They'd need a truck to do that, anyway. Up comes a plainclothes police officer. I'm not nervous, I'm not doing anything wrong. He checks my papers, the manifest. I opened the truck for him. He opens a box, pulls out a VHS tape. No tape inside, just a brick of heroin."

Sal whistled.

"I can't even tell you how angry I got. It wasn't anger. It was rage, seething rage. I saw the whole thing at once: my shit life growing up, Mireille, the Maserati, the one good thing I ever had going for me turned against me. Used to move drugs and thrown out like a dirty diaper. Under my own name, too. The manifest, everything. That was the deal, to help me make a name for myself, the New York guys had said. I can see now why they liked me. If anyone asked how I could afford the drugs, they'd say I'd sold a Maserati. And you know that if I tried to tell my side of the story, rat on these guys, that was it. One way or the other, I'm dead.

"I see the cop in front of me, staring at me, trying to figure out what my next move is going to be. Then this rage. You imagine it a thousand times in your life, just letting your rage rip, beating someone to a pulp. But that feeling goes away after a while. It didn't there. All I saw was prison, my life ending behind bars.

"He flinched, or got distracted by a sound from somewhere else, I don't remember. I pulled the gun from behind my back, where I had it tucked into my belt. He pulled out his gun, too, but I was quicker. Into his gut. It took him a while to die. I don't like that part. I don't like thinking about that.

"All that anger just fell out of me, like it had all gone into the bullet. I couldn't move. My muscles went soft. I heard his partner coming around, but not what he said. It was all murmurs, like the way you hear people in the next room, from there to intake and all the way to my conviction. When the judge's gavel came down, I knew where I was, I knew the situation, but it was the first time I'd had a clear sense of reality in months.

"That's it, gentlemen. One hot minute. And now I'm staring at this stupid rock. This is my life now. This is the rest of my life."

Whatever the guys said next came into my ears like murmurs, just like after I had killed the cop. My eyes burned with hot tears, and I began pounding the rock with my fists. "Why is this my life? Why is this my goddamned life?"

One or more of them held me back, and all I heard was, "Don't let him break his hands." Someone wrapped his arms around me, held me to his chest, and it took me a few minutes to realize it was Prosper.

18

The guys let me call the place Mireille's Neck, and we moved on. By evening, after three more hops, we found ourselves atop a deep ravine cut by a river. The plan was to descend in the morning and follow that river to its source. That might make a good place to do more serious planting, maybe some real living. Where we had landed, up above, it was a gently rolling plain of bare rock all the way to the horizon.

After a glorious blood-orange sunset, I stayed outside. The sun was most definitely a pear shape. We could see that during the daytime, too. When the bulk of this oddly shaped sun had passed below the horizon, it became clear to me, even before Bel could make his official scientific pronouncement, that we had two suns. A smaller or more distant one was emerging from behind. We were in a binary star system.

While Bel went on about all the different things this meant for us on Lapis Elpis, orbiting Gogmagog, I looked up. Gogmagog was almost directly above us, as we were closer to the equator. Its western half glowed blue, green, and gold with the sun. In the middle of the night, our shadow would creep across its belly, like it did every night. At some point, though, maybe even tonight, we would be two shadows, one cast by each sun.

The sky turned dark quickly after sunset. Lightning flashed on the far horizon, toward the northeast, though there were no clouds directly above us. We all hushed. I counted. No sound came.

"This planet is so quiet," I said. "Not even the lightning makes noise."

"That's a bit beyond the horizon, I would say," Launce said. "Five miles or more for the thunder to reach us."

"You don't even hear the wind blowing," I said.

"There's no leaves for it to blow through," Prosper said. "That's for us to do. Plant some leaves to give this rocky moon some song."

"Sing it, brother," Launce said.

"Isn't this our first storm we're seeing?" Sal said. "Our first lightning, our first rain?"

No one spoke while we searched our minds, and when each of us realized what Sal had said was true, there was no need to answer. We'd had whirlwinds and tsunamis at sea, but no rain or thunder, and nothing but calm since we had landed.

We watched one storm pass, then another, just beyond the horizon, for two hours. Launce and Prosper sang sad songs. Sal passed around the whisky bottle until it was gone. We lamented not having a fire—nothing to burn, nothing to crackle.

"Think about that," Cricket said. "How used are we to burning oil and gas? Our ancestors made fire for ages. Here, it's going to be all we can do to work up toward fire again, logs we can burn."

"We'll be long dead by the time that happens," Launce said. "We'll never see it."

"We've already planted trees," Prosper said. "It doesn't take a whole human life for a tree to grow. We'll be doing this again around a crackling fire in no time. You watch."

"Well, it's lights out," Launce said. "Tomorrow's a new day. And by tomorrow, I mean later tonight. We've got a river to run. Hopefully those clouds don't come this way, so Gogmagog can give us a good glow."

With my hands on the jamb to the vestibule door, I looked back. I went into my cell and pulled out my pup tent. I had never opened it. "I think I'm going to sleep on my own tonight."

Launce looked at Bel.

"It's not that cold anymore, and y'all snore."

"What's out there?" Sal said.

Launce looked at me. "Suit yourself."

"Do you have your sleeping bag with you?" Bel said.

"Yes, Dad," I said.

When I stepped out of the vestibule again, I realized I had never said those words, not once in my entire life. All I knew about my father was what my mother had told me, which was nothing. When I asked my grandmother about it, all she would ever say was that he was dead, which I took to mean not to ask. By the time I was twelve and realized what my mother had once been, I discovered that there were questions no one in the world could answer. I'd had friends and had felt that these guys were becoming like brothers, but I had never thought any one of them could be a father to me. They were old enough—Cricket, Bel, Sal, even Prosper—but we were all on the same level. All this passed through my mind while I set up my tent. Once inside, after I rolled out my sleeping bag, still steeped in bit of whisky, I lay down and fell asleep.

***

I woke up, sometime later, under the full green glow of Gogmagog. In a dream, or a flash of a dream, I had seen lightning breaking over the pup tent. But there could be no clouds under a bright glow like this. The earlier storms and the good feeling of watching them with the guys had given me some peace after laying out my hard truth in the morning.

A sound tickled my ears. This bothered me because there were no sounds on Lapis Elpis apart from the whirr of the module and snoring inside the dome tent, which I could hear, intermittently, from a hundred yards away. If it was raining, I would hear it falling on the tent before I heard all the raindrops gathered out there.

I shot upward. The rain out there. We were near the rim of a ravine. A low point. I struggled to open the zipper on the tent. I finally poked my head through and saw, reflecting the blue-green light from above, a stream of water rushing past the low hill on which I had chosen to sleep. It was not a hill so much as a flat belly of rock. The storms of an hour or two ago were sending a flash flood this way. There was no grass, bush, or tree to stop it.

Without lacing my boots, I grabbed my sleeping bag and

slipped out of the tent. The module was on a lower elevation, and the water was already to the bottom of the vestibule door. I still had a few feet of hill left before the water reached me. They did not.

"Yo," I called. "Launce. Bel. Sal. Prosper. All y'all, wake up. Randall. Cricket." I kept calling.

The rubber yellow hull inflated. Whether Launce had done this or the Ardeen had done it automatically, it did not matter. They were fine. They would float. Then they would hover over and get me.

I had a foot of dry land left. The water was rising fast. The module started floating away. I called out for them to get me.

No lights went on in the cell windows, and the dome tent stayed up. They were sleeping through the whole thing, thick on Sal's whisky. Cricket did not drink, and he was a light sleeper.

"Cricket. Cricket. Cricket," I kept calling.

The rushing water was at my feet. My boots started slipping.

"Think, Shelton. What is the smartest thing to do?"

The water was rushing toward the ravine. I would be swept away with it soon.

I dropped the sleeping bag and let the water drag the tent out of my hands. In winter jacket and pants, I swam with the current toward the can. The water was freezing. It was not hard to catch up to the module, but I had no good hold on the rubber hull. I straddled it with arms and legs. Water rushed over my face, and I could not breathe. My being attached to it, like a sea anchor, made the module turn, and I was behind it. If I kept crawling forward along the hull, I would reach the vestibule door, but I would have no way of reaching as high as the handle without losing my grip on the hull. I leaned my face against the hull so I could point my mouth upward and breathe. If the can lifted off the water, I might not be able to hold on. Or we might go four hundred feet up, like we usually did. Or the hover engines would burn my arm.

Lapis Elpis made my decision for me, scraping me off the hull with a sharp rock. The module floated away. Then it fell off the edge of the ravine. I was going that way, too. I scrambled but had no hold anywhere. I fell off the ravine.

I plunged into a pool. My feet hit bottom. I started coming up, and the side of my body the rock had scraped off the hull hit hard against a rock ledge. The water was trying to scrape me off this rock, too, but I could not let it. The flood would send me over another waterfall somewhere, and I would not survive it. Clinging to the rock like a spider, I slowly crawled upward. I told myself I would breathe again soon, once I broke the surface, that I could wait another minute. One knee up, then another. I did break the surface, and I did breathe again. The water did not rise higher, but it did crush hard. I would have to wait for an entire storm to scrape across my back before I budged. And I did.

I do not know how long it took, ten minutes or an hour, because every second was excruciating. If the water was not going to cover my mouth, it was going to squeeze my belly against the rock so I could not breathe. Every breath was work.

Then, after a while, it was not. The water calmed. Under

the light of Gogmagog, I saw a sloping shore of rock behind me. There was no ledge onto which I could pull myself, so I had to crawl along the rock, against the current, to get to the sloping shore. Eventually I did.

My body took its own breaths when I sat down, long and sharp. My body shook. I trembled from shock or cold; I did not know. I cried; this I knew.

It had been warm enough to sleep in my dry winter gear, but it was too cold to sit in wet wool and goose feathers. I had to find warmth even before the guys found me. I had to move.

The pool was enclosed on three sides. Water drained from the fourth side, a cliff. The rock to which I had been clinging while the water had surged past me was only a few feet from the next waterfall. I had fallen about thirty feet into this pool. The other sides of the pool were nearly vertical. The beach of broken rocks I was on butted up against one of them.

I stood, and my knees buckled, and I stood again. I leaned against the wall, and my feet slipped on the loose rocks. I walked upward this way until I felt sand. There was a swath of sand at the base of the wall. It was dry. The water had not risen this high. I pulled away loose rocks and dug a trench in the sand with my hands. I took off my boots, my coat, and my thick winter pants. They were so heavy with water I could hardly lift them. With shaking hands, I fumbled through the pockets of the coat for chemical warming packets. I found them and set them on the sand. I lay in the sand trench and pulled the dry sand on top of me. I shook, and I breathed a few grains of sand, but I lay like a mummy. The warming packets heated my butt and spine.

Gogmagog stared at me from above, his ugly face half hidden behind the wall of the pool. He waited, with dumb curiosity, to see what this creature was. The gas giant did not know what an animal was, that it lived and that it died. He did not know that this animal was about to die. He stared with no judgment, not even knowing he should expect anything different from what he saw. That was God to me. I was a whiff of piss in the alley behind his temple. When I disappeared, the eternal child would forget I had ever existed. When my flesh melted into this sand and grew mushrooms, He would not know anything else should ever have been there.

The warming packets made everything warm. My muscles softened. Even the sand seemed to burn a little. I fell asleep.

***

I woke up to daylight. That meant I had been asleep for over thirty hours. Impossible.

The water was calm in the pool. The sand was dry but cold, and I started to shiver again. My jacket, pants, and boots were not where I had left them, strewn alongside my sandy bed, the place I had expected to serve as my grave, where my rotting corpse would spread life in this watery pool.

I looked behind me. My clothes were folded neatly, and the laces of my boots were tucked in. I relaxed. The guys had been here. They would still be around. I rolled out of the sand, brushed off my thermal underwear, and put on my pants, boots, and jacket. They were dry, completely dry. The air, just above freezing, should not have let them dry, not even after thirty hours. I knew that from mistakes I had made while collecting up north.

The only safe way out of this chasm was up, and the only way up was next to where the waterfall had been last night. Launce would call it a stairway to heaven, the pile of boulders I had to climb. I scrambled over the rocks, careful not to lodge a boot in any gap. This was tiring. I was still exhausted, even after thirty hours' sleep. There was no way the chemical warming packets had lasted that long.

I came to level ground, the same level from which I had fallen last night. There were puddles everywhere, and between them slithered sandbanks that had not been there when we had landed yesterday. Just like that, after one storm, could a landscape change so much? I did not see the module—but a noise or a feeling turned me around.

On the other side of the pool was a ragged rock of a hill. This was what had diverted the water, or much of it, into the chasm. The module could be on the other side. But the feeling that had turned me around was like the feeling I'd had about the barn, where I had found the Maserati. A stream was still trickling into the pool, so I found a place to ford it, to hop over and see what was on the other side of the hill.

Someone was standing there, about a hundred yards away, in full winter gear. I waved. They nodded. As I walked, two things made the person look strange to me: they were shorter than any of the guys, shorter than me, and their winter coat, the same orange-colored coat I had, whose fur-lined hood was over their head, ran all the way to the ground. Our coats were long but not that long. Only Bel wearing Randall's coat could come close to the way this looked. Their hands were in their coat pockets.

It was a woman. Not only was I saved, but we had made contact. The signal had been sent.

"Good morning," I said. "Are you from Module One?"

"Good morning, Shelton," she said. This was a slightly older woman. Her voice was calm and confident.

"Dr. Huntsman?" I said, walking toward her.

She smiled. "Not exactly."

"Where are you from, then?"

She pulled her bare hands from her pockets and held them out in welcome. "From reality."

I stopped. I wanted to look around and see what kind of trap this was, but I also felt if I turned away from her, she would disappear and I would never see her, or anyone else, again. "Am I dead?"

Her smile faded but not completely. "Do you feel dead?"

"I'm not sure I've ever really felt alive," I said.

"Ah, you are wise," she said. "Come."

She was standing on a patch of dry volcanic sand. Up close, her face was so clear. Every line, every curve of her eyes and nose and mouth, she held out like a welcome embrace. I had seen this on people before but not to this degree, where you could look at their face and feel safe, welcome, loved. My mother's face had been like that, at least for me. Other people, no matter how nice they were, would not let you rest your eyes on their face, or their face was a blur, a kaleidoscope, a disconnected set of parts. She let me look at her. She looked like my mother but also not like her, as if my mother had some secret twin who had never done the things my mother had done, who had never had those sins written so clearly on her face. My mother's smile had been her way through the memory of her sins. This woman's smile made it seem like she had never had any, and yet it was not naïve.

"What's next, ma'am?"

"Why don't you see what the sand offers you?"

I squatted and began running my fingers through the sand to see if a diamond or a chunk of lapis lazuli would come up. I spread my feet and searched some more. I looked up at her, and without impatience or criticism, she looked down at me. This went on for a few minutes. The sand offered me nothing.

I stood up. "There's nothing in the sand, ma'am."

"That's correct, Shelton, at least the way you used the word 'in.' Here, hold your hands together, like you're praying."

I held my hands out, palms upward, in the position I had seen Prosper praying so often. "I've never prayed, ma'am."

She said, "Put the keys to the lock." She took my hands and pressed them together. There was no trickle of electricity, like when Doris Huntsman had held my hands, just warmth.

She bent over and scooped up sand in both hands. The front hem of her winter coat lifted up, and I could see that her feet were bare.

The woman then took the scoop of sand and poured it over my folded hands. The thin stream of sand pouring out from her hands fell into the small gap between my hands.

I felt the sand press against my palms. The sand kept coming and did not stop, not after all that she had scooped up should have poured out. Pressure increased on my palms, and she kept pouring. The sand was heavy and growing heavier. I did not want to stop whatever magic she was working, but the weight was becoming too much to bear. My hands shook, and some sand spilled over the sides from where she poured.

"Ma'am…."

She stopped pouring, wiped a few grains of sand from her palms, and held my hands. The weight was gone. "Now, open your hands."

On the palms of my hands, a thousand tiny grains of sand sparkled like they were each a star in the night sky. I held a universe in the palms of my hands.

"What is in the sand?" she said.

"Everything," I said.

"Everything, but not yet, Shelton Keyes. Do you understand your life now, and why you're here?"

I looked at her. I did not understand.

She pulled my head toward her and kissed my forehead.

I saw it all, at once. There was not a word in the English language, or any language, that could describe the beauty that awaited this place, this bare gray rock, this grain of sand in the infinite darkness and the millions more like it in the universe, a beauty prepared for it just by my being here. It was a million grains of gold dancing around each other in musical harmony.

When she let go, I saw a little sadness in her eyes. "Do not worry about Sal."

I heard the whirring of the module coming out of the ravine and turned to find it. When I faced forward again, the woman was gone. I turned right and saw that the sun had quickly set. The module hovered in front of me, with the dome tent still up and the rubber hull inflated. Gogmagog was glowing above. It was nighttime again. The glittering in my hands had not faded.

Prosper opened the door of the module. "You alright, Keyes?"

"Yeah," I said. "I need to save this sand. Do you have a plastic bag?"

"You hit your head, too?"

"What?"

The rubber hull deflated.

"Sal's hurt," Prosper said. "It is time to regroup."

PART FOUR

SACRIFICE

19

Prosper, after watching me stare at my hands for a few seconds, went back into the module and returned with an empty seed packet. I very carefully scraped the sand off my hands into the envelope, folded the top, and put it into my pocket.

"Alright, now," Prosper said. "Let's get a good look at you."

Inside the well-lit vestibule, Prosper gently turned my head one way and another. "Do you remember hitting your head?"

I told him what had happened.

He rubbed his face with his hands.

"One of those two things happened, Keyes. Either you swam and grabbed the module and got wet, or you stayed high and dry during the flood. And seeing as your clothes are dry, I think it was you watched us float away. Not some magical lady doing your laundry. Or maybe you got hit by lightning."

"I think I hurt my side," I said.

I unzipped my winter coat. It hurt my left side to take it off, and I could not. I could not raise my left arm. Prosper gently pulled the coat down my arms and did the same for my thermal undershirt.

"No scrapes, no bleeding," he said. He pressed his hand to my ribs. Searing pain shot up and down. "You have cracked ribs. You said you crawled up rocks? That must have been adrenaline. The same thing that kept you warm and made you see the woman."

"I really did see her."

"Alright, Keyes. We're not going to talk about that now. Let's get you strapped in to your seat."

"What happened to Sal?"

"The flood took us by surprise. We were all sleeping up top and only woke up when the module landed in the river, down in the ravine. We all scrambled to get into our cells. The module slammed into the canyon wall right when Sal was mostly down his ladder. He hit his head against the hatch opening. He's unconscious now."

"Well, the lady said not to worry about Sal. He'll be fine. I'm sure he just needs time."

"I hope you're right about time. But no more talk about this lady. Listen, we're all on a hair trigger here. Sal is dying maybe, and it's stressing out Launce and everyone else. Talking about hallucinations is only going to add to the pile. You get me, brother?"

I leaned my head back against the wall of the vestibule and grimaced.

"Let's get you into your cell, then."

Prosper held my hips while I ascended the ladder into the dome tent. I could only reach my right arm above me. Once I was able to plant my arm on the upper deck, Launce pulled me the rest of the way while I stepped up the ladder. Prosper's hands on my hips kept me from falling, since my feet slipped off the rungs a couple of times. Prosper climbed down into my cell first and held me again while Launce lowered me. Prosper strapped me into my seat and put a moistened Hidden Rat wafer and a cup of hot coffee on the small table next to the computer screen. While he was preparing all this, I heard Launce and Cricket talking about the dome tent. Bel and Randall were in Sal's cell. I could hear them through the intercom.

"I'm not a doctor, Randall. None of us are. We just have to wait and see."

"So he dies?"

"No one is saying that. It might be a concussion."

"Don't we have medicine?"

"Not for this, Randall. Not for anything this serious."

"They just want us to die."

Bel sighed. "This is a death sentence, remember?"

"But it's our life now. It's our life now."

"Stay here with Sal. Keep him company. He likes you, liked you from day one."

I heard Randall's heavy, tear-laden groans through the intercom. I spoke to Prosper. "Sal's made it this far, what, seventy hours now?"

"What do you mean, 'seventy hours'?"

"I told you, I woke up during the daytime. I thought it was thirty hours, but it must have been closer to seventy, because the sun set again when the lady left."

"Man, you just hold tight with all that, alright? It's been about two hours since we went to bed and twenty minutes since we got control of the module again. It has not been a whole day."

"How are my clothes dry?"

"I don't know, kid. Maybe the lightning. Eat a little. Have some coffee. Or just try to sleep. It's going to be a long night. I'm going to go help Launce and Cricket fix the dome tent. Just holler if you need anything."

I heard, through my open hatch, Bel and Launce arguing.

"It's a bent rib," Launce said. "The best way to fix it is to put the dome tent down. The other ribs will straighten it up. But if you try to straighten it yourself, you're only going to put smaller bends in it, and we won't be able to close the tent at all. Just you and Cricket hold the fabric tight where I need to lay down some duct tape."

This went on for an hour. I could not sleep with my sharp, pained breathing. Each breath stung my side. The only thing to do for a cracked rib was to wait. On Earth, it would have been the same remedy: time. Not so for Sal. Time was against him here. Sal was a victim of his circumstances, our first victim. Or, not a victim; this was a death sentence. Huntsman had said so before we left. Sal was suffering and would suffer more until he died. The best thing might be to put Sal out of his misery, and ours.

***

"I don't agree with that," Prosper said.

We were discussing what to do, each from our cells.

"Is this some kind of religious scruple?" Bel said.

"It's about life," Prosper said. "The man still has it. There's no saying he's suffering right now."

"I don't agree, either," Randall said. "He can still live."

"You see?" Prosper said.

"We could vote on it," Bel said.

"You aren't going to vote on whether a man lives or dies," Launce said. "One way is right. We've just got to figure it out."

Cricket typed in a chat window, *This is about keeping all of us alive.*

"What do you mean, Cricket?" Bel said.

Hush, Cricket typed.

Sal and Randall were not included in the chat group.

You know what I mean. Sal dies and who knows how the big man reacts. Especially if we kill him.

Prosper raised his eyebrows. Bel rubbed his.

"Randall, you stick with Sal, alright? You tell us how he's doing," Launce said.

"You're not going to kill him," Randall said.

"No, we're not," Launce said. "End of discussion. Let's all just hang tight. Shelton's hurt, too. Come daylight, we'll find a place to hunker down for a while."

***

The aspirin, one of the few medicines the IOSS had given us, kicked in. We had only basic first aid kits. There had been nothing in Sal's kit to help him. He had not broken the skin, so no gauze or tape was necessary. Launce had made a makeshift neck brace out of Sal's winter pants in case he had broken it. The line between healing and dying was becoming pretty clear. I was going to live. Sal was going to die.

The lady, though, she had told me not to worry about Sal. There was no way I had made her up. She had been the most real thing I had ever seen. Maybe she had meant not to worry if Sal died. We would all die, eventually. And Sal's decaying corpse would give life to this world.

The medical guide in the computer told me it would be six weeks to heal a cracked rib. Seven days, Lapis Elpis time. That was seven long days of solitary confinement in this cell, or however long it took before I could climb out again without help. There was not much I needed to do outside, anyway, except stare at bare rocks.

The aspirin took the sharpness out of the pain in my side. I slept off and on.

***

It was a long night made longer by the aspirin wearing off and our worrying about Sal. Prosper broke into prayer every few hours. Launce hummed sad mountain songs. Bel and I could not focus on our chess games though we did entertain ourselves for a little while by trying to make the worst moves possible, which ended up teaching me more than all my attempts at deep strategizing and memorizing openings. That was all of us on this mission, a collection of the worst moves possible. Cause enough chaos, and some order would emerge from it.

As soon as light trickled into the eastern sky, Launce had us airborne. He said nothing as he flew the Ardeen, but I think we all understood the path. We were in the ravine, going downstream. The river would eventually widen and slow down in some valley. And it did.

It took two hops for us to find what we were looking for: broad, sandy banks at a bend in the river. Loose rocks and volcanic sand littered the easy slope and plains beyond. We cast a vote from our cells.

"It's unanimous," Bel said. "We stay here. No more hops."

"Well," Launce said. "We'll have exploratory missions."

Bel was silent.

"Once we're settled," Launce said.

Launce set us on the inside of the bend, on a low rise.

"The sand is on the other side of the river," Prosper said.

"Yep," Launce said. "Better to keep certain things separated, if you catch my drift."

Gotcha, Prosper wrote.

I could only listen from my cell as the guys put up the dome tent and went outside to walk around. They did the courtesy of opening my hatch. Through the window, I could see Randall walk straight to the river, whose water he tasted and approved. Bel designated the upstream part of the bend as our drinking supply and the downstream part of the bend as our bathing and washing area.

"Home sweet home," I said with only comatose Sal listening through the intercom, and I slapped the wall of my cell.

20

"Big Bend," Cricket said.

"That's...no," Launce said.

"How about simply Home?" Bel said. "Casa Nostra?"

This was another round of arguing over what to name our chosen place. We had just woken up from our daytime sleep. Because I had not been sleeping well, I had been awake for the midday eclipse. The sky was brighter because the smaller sun was very distinct from the larger one now and shined for a few minutes before passing behind Gogmagog.

"Hey, we've got to name our two suns, too," I said. It hurt to holler up into the dome tent, but there were no intercoms up there.

"Fat Man and Little Boy," Bel said. He then had to explain that those were the names of the first two nuclear weapons ever used in war. "All stars are nuclear."

"I'll let it stand, for now," Launce said.

"Oh, you'll let it stand," Bel said.

"Come on, now," Prosper said.

"Cue Ball and Pocket," Cricket said.

"Now we know how you spent your life on Earth," Prosper said. "That makes Gogmagog the eight ball. Big black eight ball in the sky. Sounds like an old blues song."

"I could use an eight ball right now," Launce said. "Now you know how I spent my life on Earth."

I was stuck in my cell, and it hurt my ribs too much to speak loudly enough for the guys upstairs to hear me. I felt like a child in a room full of adults.

"Who let one go?" Bel said.

Mostly adults.

"Wasn't me," Prosper said. "Randall?"

"He's outside, throwing rocks," I said.

"Then, it was you down there, Keyes," Prosper said.

"Please," I said and winced.

"Hold on a sec," Launce said.

I heard some movement and saw Launce appear on Sal's video screen. He put his fingers to his pulse. Launce hung his head then turned to look up through the hatch. He said, "It was Sal."

I closed my eyes and lay my head back.

"That's good news, right?" Prosper said.

"I'm afraid not," Launce said.

No one said anything. I knew they were trying to figure out how to break the news to Randall.

"Hey," I said to Launce over the intercom. "Maybe Sal just needs a little sunshine. To heal, right?"

"Yeah, that's right. Good one."

I heard the guys shuffling about and saw what I could through the camera. Prosper and Launce pulled Sal from his chair and held his arms up to Bel and Cricket, who pulled him up into the dome tent and lowered him into the vestibule. Through my window, I could see the guys carry Sal from the vestibule to the bank of the river and lay him down. Prosper looked back in my direction. I heard them faintly, whatever the intercom in the vestibule picked up.

"Listen, Randall," Launce said, with his lanky arms crossed, "the reason we wanted to bring Sal out here is that he's already gone. Already passed away. Uh…."

Randall turned around and stared into the river. He said something I could not hear.

"We all hate this place," Bel said. "But if you or he had never come, you never would have known each other." He put his hands in his pockets and fidgeted on his feet.

Randall squatted down and ran his hand through the water.

"So, maybe you could help us pull Shelton up, and we can all have a proper funeral for Sal," Launce said.

Randall stood and faced the guys. "What do you mean?"

Prosper and Cricket very subtly braced one foot behind themselves and slowly freed their hands from their pockets. They saw something in Randall's eyes I could not from this distance. Launce pretended to be distracted as he also took up a defensive position.

"What do you mean?" Randall said, thrusting his arms in the air. "What do you mean?"

Launce put up his hands. "We just mean we should give him a proper burial."

Randall held his arms wide and said, "Where? With what? We dig in the rocks?"

"Across the river, you know? There, in the sand," Launce said.

Randall had squatted down again and was picking up softball-sized rocks. "How about with these?"

"Now, that's not a bad idea," Cricket said.

Randall threw one of the rocks at Cricket. "Shut up, faggot."

Prosper and Launce rushed at Randall, but he shook them loose and stepped forward and punched Cricket in the side of the head. "Sal told me about you."

I could only see Cricket's boots. He was on the ground, not moving.

Launce and Prosper tried to grab hold of Randall again, but he backed away and pointed at them, warning them away. Randall backed into the river and swam to the other side. He walked up the opposite bank and kept going, out of sight.

Bel was kneeling next to Cricket. Launce said something to Bel. Prosper was still staring at Randall, who was coming in and out of view as he passed over the rocky plain. Launce said something to Prosper. Prosper wailed.

"Not this way. Not this way," Prosper yelled. "It didn't have to be like this. We're all free here."

Bel knocked on my window. "Do you think you can manage to climb out?"

"Don't bring Keyes out," Launce said. "If Randall comes back, he's in no shape to fight or even run."

"Randall isn't coming back," Prosper said. "Neither is Sal. Neither is Cricket. Damn. Goddamn. Jesus. Je–sus." He bent over and cried. He arced upward and wailed again.

I did not want to see what Randall had done to Cricket with just one punch. I had seen enough dead bodies in my life. I did not want to see the faces of two men I had just seen alive as empty masks of flesh. Bel's expression told me to come. I nodded. He helped me up and down the ladders of our cage with more strength than I had given the old man credit.

Holding my side, I walked over to Cricket. He looked like he was taking a nap on the rocks.

"Why'd you bring Keyes out?" Launce said. "We've got to bury these guys on the other side of the river anyway and hover over there. Come on. Let's do this quick. Randall might come back, and we should be gone by then."

I sat with my feet dangling over the edge of the open vestibule door while we hovered across the river. For the second time on this mission, I shared the vestibule with two dead bodies. Sal still smelled from when he had released his sphincter. We landed, and Prosper came down.

"Take a look," I said.

Sal's head was on Cricket's shoulder, and Cricket's head was resting on Sal's.

Prosper put his arm around my shoulder. "Praise God, Keyes. Praise God. These two men are going to spend the next million years next to each other in peace, their bodies giving life to this wretched place. Until they rise from the dead, like the good Lord promised." He sniffled, wiped his cheek, and pounded his fist into his palm.

Launce and Prosper dug the graves. Bel put a ration wafer in each man's mouth to pay Charon's obol and to have the probiotics help the men's bodies fertilize the land. When everything was ready, we stood over their bodies in the graves.

"Good Lord," Prosper said. "We just want to thank you. You have brought us this far. You have kept us alive in this inhospitable place for much longer than we could have expected, and longer than we certainly deserve. We commend to you Sal Combes and Cricket St. Clair. You took them from us, one way or another, and we give them back to you and hope you let their bodies give life to this place you have created. Forgive their sins. And forgive us ours. Forgive Randall and bring him home safe so we can continue our journey together. Amen."

After a rendition of "Amazing Grace," we shoveled sand on top of the two bodies and covered the sand with as many of the loose rocks as we could find before dousing the graves with water from the river.

"That's it," Launce said.

"Now what?" I said. "We going or what?"

"You want to wait for Randall to come back?"

"What if he messes with the graves, you know?" Prosper said. "Shouldn't we be here?"

"He's got no food with him," Bel said. "He'll have to come back soon."

"If he comes back, I'm going to kill him," Launce said. "It's only right."

"You'll kill him if we leave with his food," Prosper said.

"He made that choice," Launce said.

"We leave his food and his gear," Prosper said. "Let him do like Degory and make his own way."

"Are we recharged yet?" I said.

Launce threw his shovel back in the module. "No, Keyes,

we are not recharged yet. Not for a full hop. We'll make it back across the river and then some."

"So," Bel said, "we go back across the river and keep an eye out. If Randall looks like he's going to cause trouble, we warn him off. If not, he stays."

"I'm not sharing another minute in this module with that monster," Launce said.

"I think we can all agree on that, right?" Prosper said. "We pack his kit and leave it outside, across the river. He comes any closer than that, and we knock him back into the river with the can. What choice we got?"

Launce put his hands on his hips and said, "Fine. What choice do we have? But the kid keeps first watch."

That was me. I was seven years younger than Launce, therefore a kid. With Randall and Degory gone, I was the youngest by far.

I walked around. It hurt too much to climb the ladder.

Gogmagog began to glow with the late afternoon sun, pale stripes of white and gold, the only colors that came through the turquoise sky. The second sun, Little Boy, was separating from Fat Man more with each passing hour.

Launce took the Ardeen up a few hundred feet to scan the landscape for Randall. "No joy," he said when he came down again.

"We should name this place," I said, sitting on the edge of the vestibule.

"Yeah," Launce said. He leaned against the can.

"River Rest," I said.

"Maybe."

"And this river, too. Rio Real." That was my way of sneaking in a reference to Lady Reality, who had visited me on top of the ravine this river was carving through the rock.

"Why not just plain old Royal River?" Prosper said, walking toward us from wherever he had gone to walk off today's events. "You fellows like foreign names for some reason. It says it better in English. We've just buried the first two kings of Lapis Elpis here."

"Valley of the Kings," I said. "That's what we call it."

"What time do you guys have?" Bel said, ignoring me.

"Last I checked, the vestibule said thirty-three o'clock," I said. "Come on: Valley of the Kings."

Bel looked toward the setting suns. "It can't be just our latitude."

"Maybe *what's* our latitude?" I said. "You talking about losing time again?"

"We're at six degrees south now. There's not much difference in a day from eight degrees south, where we were yesterday." Bel looked across the river. "We're an hour short of a day, and the suns are about to set. I like Valley of the Kings." He walked back into the module.

The suns did set earlier than usual, by more than an hour. During the night, Gogmagog looked bigger than normal, too. Our double shadow raced across its surface in less time, two and a half hours. The next morning, the two suns rose much earlier, by a full four hours.

"Now what?" I said, right after sunrise.

Bel said, "Now I share my theory."

21

"It goes like this," Bel said. He was sitting on a large rock. The suns had just risen.

I was sitting on the sill of the open vestibule door not far from him. Launce was leaning against the Ardeen, his arms crossed. Prosper was tossing a rock between two hands.

"The IOSS was absolutely certain we would not be facing any foreign lifeforms. Yet they were completely uncertain where in space and time we would end up once we passed through the portal. They were convinced that our being here—wherever this is—as biological lifeforms would send a signal back to Earth. Create conditions for others to follow. So, here it is: I think we created this place."

Launce sighed vigorously. Prosper, still tossing his rock back and forth, cast a hard glance at Bel.

"Can I say something?" I said.

Prosper turned to me. "Not yet, Keyes."

"What's that all about?" Bel said.

"It's about the fact that it is your turn to speak," Prosper said. "Without us interrupting."

"Alright, then," Bel said. "The death of two of our company just took five hours off the day."

"We don't know that yet," Launce said. "It'll take a few days to figure out what's going on."

"Fine. But what happened when we arrived?" Bel said. "We were headed toward Gogmagog, about to die. Something happened, and we got drawn into the gravitational pull of this moon, Lapis Elpis. Where we've been living in relative safety until recently. A moon perfectly suited for us in mass, atmosphere, and temperature."

"It's a lot colder than I would like," Prosper said.

"But bearable," Bel said. "And there's more. The atmosphere on this moon was really just hydrogen and oxygen when we first encountered it, when we first started falling in. But when Ash and Willand turned the module, our engines set the air on fire. You remember the serpents of fire?"

"How can anyone forget?" Launce said.

I had forgotten about that until this moment after all the other weird stuff we had faced.

"That fire became water. We came up through the sea because the water was all around us."

"What about the land, the ocean floor?" I said.

"Which was hot," Bel said. "The ocean was hot. I think this moon was a burning hot meteor or asteroid that Gogmagog had somehow already turned to molten magma, and which escaped the gas giant and took some of its gas with it. But that's pure speculation."

"A thieving moon," Prosper said. "I'm down with that."

"Right. I get it. And we got here at exactly the right moment for this to be exactly the kind of place we could live," Launce said. "Sounds too coincidental to me. I think the IOSS knew exactly where they were sending us and just couldn't say. You don't land on a place like this by sheer luck."

I said, "Yeah, but we weren't even supposed to be here. Ash and Willand weren't supposed to get stuck to us. Module Nine wasn't meant to be a spaceship. So, alright, something sent us here. And I've got a theory about that, too."

"Let Bel finish, guys. Especially you, Keyes," Prosper said.

"I'm saying it is not luck or providence or coincidence that put us here," Bel said. "What I'm saying is that this world is being built around us, for us, by whatever the portal really is. The portal doesn't send you anywhere. It creates a world for you. Because Ash and Willand got stuck to us, the portal thought we were a spaceship, and it built space for us to fly through. Once it was time for us to land somewhere, this lovely moon appeared and practically opened its arms to us."

"Hey, I'm looking at two graves that say otherwise," Launce said. "What exactly are you trying to say? That we're dead already? That this is heaven or hell or somewhere in between? We've all been saying that one way or another for over a month now. But you don't die again once you're dead, and we've got two dead bodies across the river. Bel, you're stressing me out with your theory. Now, let's just see how this day goes, long or short, and then we can talk some more."

I understood why Prosper did not want me talking about the lady I had seen. Launce was ready to snap.

"Oh, damn," Prosper said.

I followed his eyes across the river, where Randall was standing, silhouetted by the small sun.

"Alright, ready and steady," Launce said. He pulled out his folding knife.

Prosper pulled out his knife, too.

I fumbled for mine and dropped it.

"Keyes, you can run the Ardeen from the vestibule," Launce said. "You get in there and use it as a weapon, needs be. Ram it against the big guy."

Randall walked between the graves and stared at them. He bent over, picked up a clump of sand, studied it, and crushed it. He ran his finger across the residue on his palm. "Ha!"

"What fresh insanity is this?" Launce said.

Randall, as if hearing Launce, looked at us. He bent down again and picked up two large rocks, one in each hand. He held them out, arms spread wide, and looked at each one. "I am Gogmagog, and these are my moons. I am the god of all space and time!"

He smashed both rocks against his own head in unison. This did not seem to affect him. He then smashed one rock, then another, against his temples, repeatedly, until his tired arms missed and he fell to his knees.

"In the Ardeen. All of us," Launce said.

Bel, Prosper, and Launce hopped in behind me. Launce made us hover forward. For the third time, I was crossing this river, the Royal River, with my feet dangling in the open. This time, though, I was first in striking distance of a psychopathic giant.

We landed. Randall did not budge. A thin stream of

blood ran from his gaping mouth. Prosper hopped out, knife ready, then Launce.

"Drop the rocks, Randall," Prosper said. "Come on now, brother."

Randall dropped the rocks, one each by the buried heads of Sal and Cricket. He pressed his hands to the mounds of damp earth around their bodies. "Don't you guys see? It's a good thing to die here. We're alive, and there's nothing else we can ever be." He fell to his side.

Launce jumped next to Randall and cut his throat. Randall's blood trickled between the two mounds that Sal and Cricket made. "I feel better now," Launce said.

"What were they expecting from us?" Prosper said. "Look at this. You send death dealers, you get dealt death. But this is what they wanted. For us to kill each other and fertilize this place for themselves. That's all we could ever be to them."

Bel studied a handful of the sand covering Sal. He knit his brow.

"What'you thinking?" I said.

"Not much, yet. But…it's not exactly what we mixed together yesterday. It's almost starting to bind."

"'I am the god of space and time,'" Launce said. "What the hell got into him?"

Bel said, "Those last words, though, those were the most articulate he had ever been. 'We're alive and there's nothing else we can ever be.'"

"Amen," I said.

"Alive? I count three dead bodies now," Launce said. "Three down in less than a day. I'm not liking this particular bend in the river anymore. I say we bury the big guy and skedaddle."

22

We buried Randall next to Sal and hovered back across the river to formulate a plan. This time, Launce hovered so low over the river that my outstretched boots briefly skimmed the water. I figured he was picking on me because he needed to pick on someone or so stressed out he could not fly right, or both. We stood in a circle near the door of the vestibule.

"I say we head for center," Bel said. "Our mapping shows the ripples in the landscape radiating out from a center near the equator."

"I don't know," Launce said. "Sounds like inviting trouble. Sounds like a trap. Listening to you talk about this place, it feels more like this moon's trying to eat us. Laying a trap. A Venus Fly Trap."

"Isn't that life?" I said.

"What do you mean?" Prosper said.

I had not meant anything by it. They were just words, something to say. They did not match my experience of the Lady. And Prosper would not let me talk about the Lady, so I did not know what he had wanted by asking me what I meant. The guys were looking at me, as if, for the first time, they wanted to hear what I had to say. So, I had to make up something.

"All I mean is, life seems to be nothing more than getting us to move things around, like we're about to do again. All our ambitions, looking for new lands, building up empires, it's just to make us move our bodies around, spread our seed. It's true on Earth, and it's true here. Death means nothing to life. It's just more life. I think that's what Randall meant, too."

"Look who's a philosopher," Launce said.

"You keep picking on me about sharing my thoughts, Launce. But look around. I'm alive with you guys now. We're still on this side of death."

"The man is right," Prosper said. "We all gotta listen to each other now. I have to say, though, that's not what I thought you were going to say, Keyes. But let me add to what you say. Maybe life and death mean nothing to a fallen world, but I believe in heaven. Up there, it all matters. What we do here matters for up there."

"Up there?" I said. "Let me respectfully disagree with you, Prosper. This is it. We're 'up there.' We traveled through space. You look up to the skies looking for God, and this is what you're looking at. This bare-ass rock. Bel here once said we were being tossed out like Earth's garbage, and I say that's what heaven is, y'all's garbage dump. You put there everything you can't handle in this life, pain and uselessness. This is where it ends up, building another world people want to flock to, so they escape this world. But this is all that's waiting for them."

Prosper looked at me calmly. Bel looked at me and then at Prosper. Launce was spaced out.

"I know where you're coming from, Keyes," Prosper said. "I really do. You're not the only one around here who came from nothing. And, so, you think life is dog eat dog for everyone. But I learned that's not the case. There are plenty of people just happy to get along, happy to give. That comes from heaven. It's not about putting away all our suffering in heaven but receiving the graces that come from there."

Launce grimaced and walked away. Bel seemed eager to be a spectator.

"No," I said, "you'll see that everyone just eats their dog a different way. Even if we're talking about happiness. People tell you their way will make you happy because it makes them feel happy. They need you to love God so they can feel good about loving God. It's a pyramid scheme. And God is the biggest dog-eater of us all. If He made all this, as you say, it's only to keep pulling us around by the nose, to make us hop from planet to planet looking for Him, because that's the only way He can be happy, making us look for Him. But here we are, just another bare rock that's only any good by our being dead on it. Bait and switch. Even God eats His dog, He just does it in a different way than us crooks. Biggest con man of them all."

Prosper kept looking at me, and I saw a defensive smile slip onto his face.

Bel looked at Prosper to hear his response.

"And how does your lady figure into this?" Prosper said. "Seems you had a different experience of life for a moment. Was that real or what?"

"The most real thing I've ever known," I said. "That wasn't about heaven or God or nothing. That was about reality. Lady Reality, I call her. Like you said, my mind made her up to keep me alive. She knows what's up, and it ain't heaven. It's wherever this body is."

Bel smiled.

"You amaze me, Shelton Keyes," Prosper said. "How you can see so much and not put it all together. Tell me again what you experienced, what you felt, when you saw what this universe was all about? It meant so much to you that you insisted you keep the sand she poured into your hands. But you won't admit there's something behind it all."

I looked at Bel. "He's referring to an experience I had after the flood."

He kept smiling. "I know, Shelton."

"Oh, so Prosper tells me to keep quiet about her but can't keep my secrets to himself?"

Bel nodded toward Launce, who was washing his face on the riverbank.

"Alright, I don't know what that was. Or how it all fits together. Maybe Bel's got a theory for that. Maybe the next one of us to die will tell another secret of the universe before smashing his own head in."

Launce walked back. "You guys ready?"

"Ready for what?" I said.

Launce slapped me on the shoulder. I winced from the shooting pain in my rib. "Let's go eat this dog, kid," Launce said. He had heard the whole conversation. Prosper had used my story of the Lady to win the argument even though he had thought Launce's hearing about the Lady would set him off. But Launce seemed fine now, even better than before.

***

Launce had himself and Prosper take new cells so the four of us who remained could balance out the weight on the Ardeen. We all had to call it the Ardeen now, Launce insisted.

Just as we were ready to go, a massive dust storm came upon us followed by thunder and lightning. Awake and ready this time, we took down the dome tent, which leaked and whose metal ribs Launce thought made too good a lightning rod. He inflated the rubber hull so the metal can we called home would not serve as a conductor.

The four of us sat in our air-conditioned cells for the rest of the day, listening to the thunder crash. Launce turned the Ardeen so he could keep an eye on the graves to make sure the Royal River did not carry away the corpses of our kings. I did not know what Launce could see because my window was fogged over.

The storm passed, and the river rose, but it did not rise high enough to sweep away our garden. The suns set. Daylight had lasted five hours less than yesterday.

Launce took us up for a night hop. The land kept up the same ribbed pattern as we went northeast. The tall, smooth ridges on which we had first landed weeks ago turned into shorter, rocky slivers of land rising between long lakes and rivers. Every ridge was lower than the one before it and made a tighter curve so that the whole continent seemed shaped like a target. The center of the continent was a bull's-eye waiting for our arrow.

When we finished that hop, we climbed out of our seats to put up the dome tent. When I poked my head through the hatch after struggling up the ladder with cracked ribs, I found Prosper, Launce, and Bel staring at something behind me. I tried to turn and see, but it hurt.

"Could I get a hand here?"

"What's different about Gogmagog?" Prosper said, ignoring me.

"It's bigger," Launce said.

"Noticeably so," Bel said.

I leaned my head backward. The ball of blue, green, and gold gas nearly filled my field of vision.

"Is this good or bad, Bel?" Launce said.

"Anyone want to help me get up?" I was staring at three pairs of boots.

"Well, let's look at the facts," Bel said. "Shorter days mean a faster orbit around Gogmagog. I'm no astronomer, but that could mean we're closer to Gogmagog than we were before. And that's why it's bigger to us."

"Did all this dying bring us closer?" Prosper said.

"It could fit my theory, but that's a question for the universe," Bel said.

"Yeah, well, it seems pretty pertinent to us," Launce said. "If we're getting sucked into Gogmagog, I want to know about it."

I said, "Don't you guys know about ecliptical orbits?"

"Elliptical orbits," Bel said. "Yes, that rings a bell now. Good one, Shelton. No worries. We're just at perigee."

"Maybe you're at perigee, but I'm stuck on this ladder. Let me up."

The next full day was fifty-two hours long, twenty-six of daylight and twenty-six of dark. The day was a deck of cards, of light and dark suits. We named the hours for the numbers, ace through king. If we were going to keep losing hours, we would think of it like tossing cards on the table.

Daylight began on diamonds and ended on hearts. The night began on clubs and ended on spades. Prosper saw something biblical in that. I did not know what I saw in it. I walked off by myself a lot, hoping Lady Reality would tell me more.

***

I woke up, later that night, at queen of spades, the twenty-fifth hour after sunset. We had one more to go before sunrise. It was dark inside the dome tent, which meant it was cloudy, and Gogmagog would only be a crescent in the sky at this hour, anyway. I climbed down without my ribs bothering me too much.

Outside, the sky was so black I felt I could cut away at it. I could not even see my feet. I was only breath in space. The planet I orbited was Module Nine, and I ran my hand along the metal hull as I walked. When I reached the other side of the can, I saw a faint red glow toward the northeast. I thought it was the first hint of sunrise, so I waited.

I waited for an hour, during which time I heard the other guys stir. The faint red glow did not change. It pulsed a little but did not change. Finally, Fat Man did rise, farther to the south, almost due east. The faint red glow had been something else. It disappeared in the daylight.

"Could be anything," Launce said once he and the others came down.

"I'm just reporting what I saw," I said.

"And I'm just analyzing your report."

Prosper helped me back into the Ardeen so we could take down the dome tent and make another hop.

"Why do you keep helping him?" Launce said once I was down in my cell. "Keyes got himself up and out this morning. Either he can or he can't. Make him pick."

"Give the kid a break," Prosper said.

I did not hear what Launce said or see his reaction. I certainly did not understand what he suddenly had against me.

Bel came on the intercom. "Just take it easy, Shelton. Don't aggravate your condition."

I texted him. *My condition is I don't know why Launce keeps picking on me all of a sudden.*

So that he feels you're the one on the edge, and not him.

Bel was exaggerating about Launce. Apart from annoying me, he seemed fine. When Degory had left, weeks ago, I had wondered who was the craziest one left. When Sal had died, that left Randall. Now that they and Cricket were gone, I could not tell whom that left.

23

Later that day, on our second hop, we began following a narrow but very deep ravine. I could not see the bottom through my window. It was a river of black. The lidar imaging said it was four thousand feet deep and growing deeper. Prosper, who was flying, veered left and right to follow it. Launce, who was lying back with his eyes closed and arms crossed, sighed audibly.

"Oh, mama," Bel said.

I soon saw what he had seen through his window. The ravine emptied into an enormous canyon, as big or bigger than the Grand Canyon. The walls were miles apart. The floor dropped away quickly more than six thousand feet.

"That's below sea level," Launce said without opening his eyes.

"We don't actually know that," Bel said. "This whole moon could be a little egg shaped."

"You're egg shaped," Launce said.

Bel bounced his eyebrows like he was relieved by the joke.

"There's water down there," I said. "You can tell by the squiggly lines on the map."

Prosper said, "Launce, you want to take us down?"

"Not really. We can't go chasing every river. There'll be no place to land down there. Keep us above the rim of the canyon." Launce did not open his eyes or uncross his arms.

We flew for a few more minutes.

"It's really very beautiful," Bel said.

Launce smacked his lips and looked out the window. "Take us down to that lake."

Prosper landed on the shore of the lake, at the flattest part he could find, but the can was slightly tilted. That made it hard for me to grab the ladders in and out of the can.

The ground was powdery red rock. The water was silver, completely still. The sky, embossed with a crescent of late-morning Gogmagog, reflected perfectly in it. The air smelled of sulfur.

Bel tested the water. "A sulfur spring. Nice and warm. Seems safe." He took off his boots, socks, and jumpsuit.

"You're going to make ripples," Launce said.

"Only at first."

Bel slid his hairy body gently into the water and floated, arms and legs splayed. Prosper and I looked at each other then joined him. Launce came in last. The four of us floated serenely in the sulfur pool. An almost sheer wall of undulating rock rose nearly seven thousand feet above us, into the turquoise sky, and just as far below us, into the mirror pool. No one spoke.

Beneath the surface, my ears took in very little. Lapis Elpis was quiet. Quieter than the death house had been. There were no dogs barking, no airplanes in the sky, no insects buzzing, no whirring of machines except the Ardeen, and that was off right now. Even the wind, without leaves or grass to play with, was always silent. Walking on this moon was watching a film on mute. With my ears under the water and my eyes closed, the only noises in the world came from me: my throat as I swallowed, the buzz of my nerves, my arms slowly churning the water.

Fat Man, the bigger sun, fell behind Gogmagog, casting the world in shades of charcoal. Little Boy was bright enough by which to see but not much more, a blue nightlight. A little while later, Little Boy joined Fat Man behind the eclipse. Lapis Elpis was left in total darkness. But not for long.

The rock began to glow. Clusters of green, pink, and purple fluoresced in bands along the undulating rock wall and in the mirror pool. When my feet pointed toward the wall, I felt I was floating in outer space. Like I was an alien or Jesus gently floating down to enter a new world. Until the two suns reappeared, I was face to face with Gogmagog. We stood toe to toe, man to man. I had another world waiting for me. The Lady had shown me. This dumb giant knew it and was doing everything he could to take me in, to eat me before I could escape. I would escape his clutches. How, I did not know. The Lady knew. The glowing rocks below my feet were a dim suggestion of what she had shown me.

We stayed long enough for a recharge. The rocks lost their glow after a while. Bel brought out his litter box, which was, like the rest of ours, now filled mostly with local sand. He mixed up the soil and sowed a few seeds he thought would do well near the sulfur lake. When he explained that sulfur was good for plants, Prosper suggested we just take some of this soil back with us.

"Back where?" Launce said.

"The Valley of the Kings," Prosper said.

Launce smiled and nodded in a weird way, like he was secretly sure that once we reached the center of Lapis Elpis, we were not coming back.

24

The next hop, taken after daysleep on the shore of Silver Lake, put our world in a new perspective. With the suns setting behind us, I stood shoulder to shoulder with Launce, Prosper, and Bel looking over the low peaks of several ragged ridges toward a volcano. It was a shield volcano, as best as Bel or any of us could identify it from forty miles away. We could see it from so far away not just because of our vantage point but because it rose into the clouds fifty thousand feet above us. It was so tall and broad it looked, near its top, like the gray rock wall that had greeted us when we had finally left the ocean. But where its top hid among thin, wispy clouds, those clouds pulsed with red light.

"This is it," Bel said. "We're at the equator. My guess is tidal forces pull magma toward Gogmagog. It builds up for a while, then *boom*."

We stood in silent awe for a few minutes until a thought found words inside my head.

"Bel, you know I'm not a scientist or nothing, but let me lay something out. So far, all the land we've seen comes out like ripples from this exact point. Do you think it's possible that this one volcano has made all the land? And if so, when this thing goes *boom*, as you say, just how big a boom are we talking about? Like those booms we heard with the tsunamis? Little booms?"

Bel shrugged. "It's all new to me, too, Shelton."

"Little booms?" Prosper said. "Those were big booms. We were just far away. Thousands of miles. Think of what kind of boom it takes to reach us half across the world."

I said, "What if it booms right now?"

"Then it's game over," Bel said.

"Damn," Launce said. "I've never seen a thing like this before. I almost want to salute it."

"Now you're like Degory," Prosper said. "Worshipping volcanos and all that."

"It's more like Mordor, if you ask me," Bel said.

Prosper, Launce, and I glanced at each other.

"Where would that be, again?" I said.

Bel dropped his head and shook it. He stayed in that position for a few minutes, much longer than I thought he should.

"You alright?"

"They'll never know our stories," Bel said. "All the life here. Imagine all the stories we have, our whole world, lost to a million years of evolution. Lost as soon as we're dead. Once the four of us are gone, that's it. No one to carry our stories forward."

"We build a time capsule," Prosper said.

"To last how long?"

"Hold on," I said. "We're here to send a signal. Other humans are coming. Nothing's lost in this place. Not yet."

"They did want us here for a reason," Launce said. "Is

this it, you think? This here volcano? If there was a goal to this adventure, this would look like it. How does this play in your theory, Bel? Did we make this volcano?"

"I don't see why," Bel said. "This moon could be filled with any number of things we need to discover or an obvious place from which to send a signal. Just our mere presence here is a miracle. In the meantime, it doesn't hurt to watch this awesome thing."

If this broad cone of charcoal-colored rock was anything, had any sense of its own being, it was speaking upward, to Gogmagog right above it in the late afternoon sky. He was pulling her upward, toward him, and she responded with words whispered on liquid red lips. She was forgetting the world around her, the children ringing her skirt, a continent formed by his invisible pull. When he let her go again, when he was done with her, she would fall to her bed, still trying to cling to him. When her lover was out of sight and just her stupid kids were left around her, that would be the time to watch out. Boom.

***

We flew the Ardeen in a broad circle around the volcano. The computer mapped the land below us in the dark while the pulsing red glow above the cloud line served as a lighthouse for us. We thought of names for the volcano. Bel played on Mauna Kea and Olympus Mons, the names of the largest volcanoes on Earth and Mars, and came up with a strange name, Mons Amusa.

"It's like Mansa Musa, the great emperor of the Sahel. Everything's being named for him in the Sahara now. You can't pass through the smallest town without seeing a Musa Burger. He had so much gold with him on a voyage to Mecca that he devalued it for decades. Like we could do with diamonds here."

"I don't see the connection," Launce said.

"He was large and in charge. Like this volcano."

"How about Hunts Mons," Prosper said. "I think that was Keyes's idea. Right?"

"Yo, we're all here because of that woman, not just me," I said. "And it was y'all who tried to name that planet above us after her until we escaped it. Not me."

"Red Hot Poker," Launce said.

"How about just Big Red?" I said.

No one answered, meaning one of them would count it as his own idea later.

It took three hours to circle Big Red from twenty miles away. The land beyond it to the north, east, and south looked, on the three-dimensional map, just like the southwest from which we had come.

"Is that it?" I said once we had landed again.

"We could try to get above, look in," Launce said. "It would take a few hops to get the Ardeen that high."

"I don't know about sleeping on the side of a volcano," Prosper said. "Sounds like inviting disaster to me."

"You hear any rumbling?" Launce said. "Any booms?"

"I see the glow of magma," Prosper said.

"You see any chunks flying out? Tell you what: the first rumblings, the first chunks, we bail. I just want to see the land-maker in person, up close. Nothing else to see on this rock. I mean, this is it, this is the center. Target acquired."

"I think this is one among many targets," Bel said. "It is certainly informative for us."

"That's all I mean," Launce said.

It was true, as the guys sometimes said, that I had much to learn about people. Anger at my own stupidity had landed me in prison in the first place. I thought I understood Launce, though, that whatever urge had led him to a capital conviction in the military was still going strong inside him—or at least the sight of Big Red had excited it again.

I texted Prosper and Bel privately: *Help us out here. He's not going to take us in, is he?*

We all have control of the module, Bel wrote. *No one can fly us in.*

God, is this how it ends? Prosper wrote.

We landed on a small shelf of black rock eight thousand feet above the base of the volcano. Bel insisted we not put up the dome tent, that we needed to be ready to run at a moment's notice, and reminded us about the flash flood that had killed Sal—as if we needed reminding.

When I opened my hatch, I agreed with him, but for a different reason. The wind went from very hot to very cold and smelled of gasses our atmospheric reader on the Ardeen told us were toxic. I had once been ready to die in a warm, clean room, lying on a padded gurney, breathing oxygen until chemicals coursing through my veins stopped my heart. I was not prepared for how suffocated I felt just being on the side of this barren volcano, still low down its slope.

***

The only thing that made boredom worse was anxiety,

and they combined to lull me into a half-nap near the end of our recharge break. Sometime during the nap, I woke up briefly to the most lucid vision of Degory staring at me from outside my window, his face lit by Gogmagog above. When the time for our hop was close, I turned on my computer screen to see who was doing what. Degory's face was front and center. I jumped in my seat.

"Degory, man, how did you get here? When did you get here?" I said. I pressed the Call Push button, meaning that the other guys, who seemed to be asleep, would hear my voice even if they had turned off their screens. "Everyone, look, it's Degory."

"The hell?" Launce said.

Prosper rubbed his face, looked around, and his big eyes grew bigger when they connected with the screen. "Hey…Degory. Long time no see."

Vamanos, Degory wrote.

"How'd you even walk all this way in the time it took us to fly?" I said.

No me detuve. I no stop. I go straight.

"Uh, so, yeah," Launce said. "We were just headed up to see the volcano, to have a look."

I know. She call you here.

No one said anything.

"You notice how the days got shorter?" I said.

No.

"We're closer to Gogmagog now."

What does this mean, Gamaga?

"The planet above us," I said.

This is Xolotl. He come and swallow us.

"Amazing," Bel said. He had finally woken up. "We separate and come up with the same myths about the planet we're orbiting."

"Yeah, that's real nice," Prosper said. "In the meantime, three of us are dead. Did you know that, Degory?"

How I know that? Come on. Vamanos. She calling us.

"Let's just hold on now," Prosper said. "We're on a scientific expedition. No one is calling us. Sal, Cricket, and Randall are dead. We've been making this journey together. None of this '*Vamanos*.'"

I looked at Launce's picture on the screen. He had been talking for days like something was calling him toward the volcano. Sending us here to this moon at all had been a way for someone or something to signal the IOSS and send others. Launce called it a target. Degory called it Chantico. That left me, Prosper, and Bel as those sane enough not to jump into this volcano. That made it three against two, but the two were crazy. Being crazy always doubled your number.

"Well," Launce said. "Maybe it is a little fate's brought us back together, and right on time. Come on. *Vamanos*."

I wrote to Bel and Prosper, Man, *I like this even less now. You're not alone*, Bel wrote. *We all have control of the can.*

***

Launce took us directly up the volcano, to forty thousand feet, where we stopped to recharge. There was little atmosphere for us up here, and opening our hatch would mean a slow, agonizing death. It was two of spades, with eleven more hours until sunrise. The next hop would still be made in darkness.

Degory challenged me to a game of chess. After all I had learned from Bel, I won quickly. Degory did not seem happy about this and would not talk to me for the rest of the four-hour break.

During the next hop, we reached the rim of Big Red. The monster of a volcano was sixty-six thousand feet tall. We circled the rim, which was five miles wide. Instead of one large lake of magma, we found several, all glowing red hot and giving off gasses we did not want ruining the Ardeen.

"Alright, we've had our look," Prosper said.

"Yep," I said.

Who first? Degory said.

"Who first what?" I said.

"No one first," Prosper said. "No one's going in."

This why we here.

"This is not why we're here. No one's jumping in a volcano. Especially no one not named Degory. There will be no pagan practices on this planet. We left all that behind on Earth."

Launce, stroking his chin, looked like he was studying the situation.

"I also vote no," I said. "If y'all can vote me into crawling through the gutter, we can vote our way out of this situation, too. We've seen the volcano, and it looks like what volcanoes look like. Aren't we all satisfied now? Bel?"

"I agree. It's time to go home."

"Where's home?" Launce said.

"The Valley of the Kings," Prosper and I said in unison. He continued, "That's our home now. That's where our brothers are buried."

"Man, nothing about this is ever going to be home," Launce said. "It's all just dumb rock."

He want to go first, Degory said.

"I said nothing of the kind," Launce said. "I just want to take a moment, if you can understand that."

I go.

"You go where?" Prosper said. "No one's jumping into this volcano. That's the end of it."

Xolotl eat us.

"Volcano eat you."

Degory put on his winter gear.

"Let's use a little logic here, Degory," Bel said. "Once you open your hatch, you're going to die. There's no atmosphere up here."

"He'd have about thirty seconds," Launce said. "Maybe more."

"Do not encourage the man," I said. "What's wrong with you? You've been sounding like you want to go in there, too."

"I've said nothing of the kind," Launce said. "But I'm also not going to tell another man what he can't do. If he wants to jump in, let him jump in."

Prosper started moving the module away from the rim. Degory was already clinging to his ladder.

"Hey now," Launce said. "We all agreed that when I'm in charge of flying, I'm in charge."

"Consider this a mutiny," Prosper said.

The two men fought for control of the module, sending us all back and forth and spinning for half a minute. Gradually, we worked our way over one small lake of magma. Degory must have seen this. He opened his hatch. The jet of escaping air tilted the Ardeen. Prosper relinquished control and let Launce right the ship. I felt a breeze coming from my vent.

"Hey, Degory's cell is sucking air out of ours. Through the gutter or something. These cells aren't totally airtight."

"Damnit," Launce said. We descended as quickly as we could, unsure if Degory was still with us or not. When we reached thirty thousand feet, Launce said, "This is the height of Everest. One of us could get out at this altitude safely and close his hatch. I'm steering."

"Not me this time," I said. "My ribs are broke."

"I'll do it. I'm right next door," Bel said. Without putting on his winter clothes, he climbed through his hatch. I saw, on screen, Bel gently drop Degory's body into his cell.

"Is he dead?" I said once Bel returned to his cell.

"I don't think so."

"He's gonna be pissed. An unworthy sacrifice. Rejected by the gods."

"Yes, he is," Bel said. "And I don't want to be there when he wakes up. He'll see it as our fault and make us the sacrifice."

"Why didn't you just dump him over the side?" I said.

"I'm not that kind of person. Besides, he'd make good fertilizer."

"Now you're thinking like Huntsman," I said.

"Seriously," Launce said. "He's gonna be a threat."

"We can't leave him up this high," Prosper said.

"We're not really just going to reject someone like this, are we?" I said.

"You were the one telling me to do it," Bel said.

"I was joking." The truth was, I did not know what I was saying, talking just for the sake of talking. I had never seen someone try to make himself a human sacrifice.

"Jokes aside, we've got to make a decision," Launce said. "I can get us down to maybe ten thousand, which is livable, especially for a Mexican. We leave all his stuff with him. Then we skedaddle. We could make the first ridge well out of harm's way. But damn if this guy doesn't walk fast."

Whatever spell the volcano had put on Launce, Degory's action had broken. We returned to our shelf of rock at eight thousand feet and left Degory where he had found us. When he woke up, if he ever did, he would think that finding us had been just a dream. While we hovered across the valley to the first ridge circling Big Red, I wondered if seeing Degory had not just been a dream for me, too.

Three hours into our recharge, up in the dome tent with the others, I felt the can shake back and forth. "Who's doing that?"

"It's Degory coming in. He's back," Prosper said.

"No way," Launce said. "He's forty miles away. One of you is just moving around too much."

"Or it's the ground itself," Bel said. "A tremor. Movement in Big Red."

I smiled. Bel had approved my choice of name.

"That would be too ironic," Launce said.

"Not ironic, not by definition," Bel said. "But statistically probable. The chances of our feeling a rumble near a volcano are as good as Randall farting after dinner, may he rest in peace. And the odds are all the better considering the way this world reacts to us. We did something, and Lapis Elpis is reacting."

No one said anything after this, and a thought took action in my limbs before it found words. I went outside and looked up. I held my hands up to measure Gogmagog. It was much bigger than it had been since Randall's death, bigger than we had seen it yesterday.

I called up through the vestibule, "It's not Lapis Elpis reacting. Gogmagog eat us."

PART FIVE

SHADOW

25

We flew for days, and the days grew shorter. Every day, we tossed four playing cards to the wind: the four kings, then the four queens, then the four jacks. One day, there would be only four aces left on Lapis Elpis, flying fast around the giant's belly.

We ran from Gogmagog, but he was always above us. At night, at each full Gogmagog, Bel held up a marked piece of paper at arm's length to measure its width. Day by day, the marks his thumbnails made crept farther apart. The day was shorter because we were orbiting faster. We were orbiting faster because we were closer to our host planet.

No matter how far we ran from Big Red, the rumblings continued. We had each taken in some combination of Bel's theory, that we were actively creating this place, and Prosper's view that were in a "Genesis moment." But we argued over whose anger was causing the rumbling and the coming demise of our world: God's, because we were crooks and killers; the devil's, because Degory could not complete his sacrifice; Lapis Elpis's, for making her clean rock and pristine water filthy with our flesh; Gogmagog's, for intruding on his neighborhood.

The closer we came to Valley of the Kings, the more we argued about what our real goal should be, what the safest place was to ride out the planet-ending earthquakes and eruptions sure to come before we ever breathed Gogmagog's blue, green, and gold gasses, what sacred site would please the angry gods above and below. Launce and Bel thought we should seek greener pastures on the open seas. The Ardeen was a submersible, after all. Prosper would go no farther than the graves of Sal, Cricket, and Randall. I agreed. I had left one certain moment of death by lethal injection and was not going to spend the rest of the life I had been offered running away from death. I would rather open my arms to Gogmagog above and enjoy one last blaze of celestial glory.

26

When the day had shortened to roughly forty hours, twenty hours of daylight and twenty hours of dark, and when we were halfway through our second daylight hop, that is, at midafternoon, Valley of the Kings, the bend in the Royal River where we had buried Sal, Cricket, and Randall, came within the horizon. None of us could see it yet from our windows, not clearly, but the Ardeen seemed almost to float on our relief. We had sown seed in many places, but the bodies of our brothers made this place home. We would soon be swallowed up by Gogmagog, and it would be in the company of those whom death had swallowed up before us.

The river's course had changed a little in the short time we had spent going to Big Red and back, which we chalked up to the seismic effects of Gogmagog's gravity. The gas giant was playing this continent like a drum. We arrived at the spot marked on the computer map and set down.

Like always, I was the last one out of the can, still struggling a bit because of my ribs. None of the other guys would help me or even answer my calls. I heard nothing from outside as I inched my way up the ladder, laid my elbows on the upper deck to rest, and completed the arduous journey to solid ground. When I did finally exit the vestibule, I saw Launce, Prosper, and Bel staring across the river. It took me a moment to understand what was different about the scene.

Green grass, knee-high, swept up the river bank on both sides. It mingled with cattails and reeds downriver as far as I could see. There was not much upriver. Beyond the growth, the rock remained bare except where grass and flowers had found foothold in cracks and crevices. I walked closer to the bank, where I could see the other side more clearly. Among the graves, or the shallow mounds that remained, a small tree had begun to sprout leaves. I bent over carefully and took a few heads of grass into my hands.

Prosper came up next to me. He took a knee and fondled the grass. He pressed a bundle to his face and began heaving. His tears poured out between his fingers. "Look what we did," came his squeaking whispers. "Look what we've done."

Launce came over, too, and wiped his cheek with the back of his hand. "They can never take this from us."

I had been expecting some kind of plant growth and did not feel what these men felt. It would be only a matter of time before we saw the grass grow up, either under our feet or between our dead bodies. I was surprised by how much of it there was after so short a time. But I was on a moon-planet that was hurling itself quickly into its nearest galactic neighbor because of our being here. So, I had been keeping my expectations open.

"Right on time," Bel said. "Figures. We get all this done, right on time for it all to be destroyed."

"Come on now," Prosper said. "Let us rejoice in this victory. Let God bless the little time we have left here."

Launce lay down among the grass. The rest of us joined him. Above us all was Gogmagog, nearly filling our field of vision: a thickening crescent of whatever of its blue, green, and gold light could penetrate the turquoise sky and a faint dark blue shadow where the rest of him lurked in the darkness of space.

"God bless you guys," Launce said, chucking a small rock in the general direction of the graves. The rock hit the water, and a breeze picked up. The breeze made the grass its instrument, a chorus of a million contended sighs. "I say we stick out here."

"You don't want to check the other sites? Clearwater Crater?"

"By the time we get there, Bel, it'll be too late," Launce said.

"We'll never know just how well we did."

"We'll know," Prosper said. "We see it already here. We'll see it again with our souls."

"How much time we got left?" I said.

Bel chuckled at something before he even said it: "All the time in the world."

Launce groaned. Prosper gave a big belly laugh.

I sat upright. "Guys, this ain't over. I don't know how, but it's not over. You guys are crying about the grass like it's the end."

"You're young, Shelton," Bel said. "I know we've said that before, but the grass means something. To see something you've made grow like this. None of us here have children, not like Sal. This is it for us. And Launce is right, it can't be taken away from us, not even by Gogmagog. It'll always be true that we did this, even if it's burned away. It is an end, the end of lives poorly lived. I was so selfish. Practically tagged along that wife of mine until I'd had enough. Never had kids because she didn't want them. These are my babies, these heads of grass. That's why it means so much, to see them before I die."

"I just mean that the Lady showed me so much more than us laying down here, waiting to die, like we were still on the gurney in the death house. Like, all this means something for the universe."

"You're young and hopeful, Shelton," Bel said. "Keep that hope alive for all of us. But I've found it better to enjoy what few and reachable things reality gives me."

"Now you sound like me before," I said.

What welled up inside me next, I could try to describe. I had called the woman Lady Reality and had boasted about my sticking to what was real around me. Hope was an idea, an abstraction, something conjured up by clergymen and movie producers to make the pain and dullness of reality more bearable. A drug. Here I was, though, speaking with hope. But it was not hope to me, not in the fairy-tale way. What I had seen was as real, more real, than the grass coming up around me and the water trickling by. "What you're calling hope I just call seeing the future like it's right in front of me. It's like, no matter what we do, the future can't be undone. It's already present."

"I hope you're right," Bel said.

"He is right," Prosper said. "I don't know about apparitions, but I do know hope. And when you feel it, it's real."

"Amen," I said and lay down again.

"Where'd you get all your faith, Prosper?" Launce said. "What's your experience?"

"Me? You know, I was living a bad way. Grew up wrong, got into gang life. Went to rob these people one day, on their compound. Got caught. They took me in, said they forgave me. I lived with them for a while on that compound. Not a cult, though. Just normal folks helping each other live. Thought I'd find a way to really rob them one day. But then I saw how they lived. It wasn't perfect, and it wasn't fake. I saw how a person could live among people without being put down, hated, looked at suspiciously. One day, they had a scandal, one of their leaders caught with his hand in the honey pot, if you catch me. I told them they were all hypocrites, and I left. Got back into it, but not with gangs. I'd had enough of living out other people's ideas. I was like young Shelton that way. That's why I said what I said before, when you first talked about reality and the lady statue. I was on my own and not too smart about it. That, gentlemen, is why I'm here. But those good people, they came to see me. Visited me in prison. Said I was their brother. And I felt it, but not in a deep way. Not until I saw just this one thing. Man, you're gonna laugh."

"Prosper, we've got a planet bearing down on us right now. I'll take a good laugh about anything," Bel said.

"Alright," Prosper said. "Owls."

"Owls?" I said.

"Owls. Picture of an owl, to be precise. It was camouflaged against a tree. You really had to look to find it. Only the open eyes gave it away. So, I sort of halfheartedly praised God for the owl, for the order of creation, for making the animal fit His environment. The balance of creation. And you see it all over, animals that really disappear into the bark and the leaves and you name it. What's the one that actually changes on the fly?"

"A chameleon," Launce said.

"That's it. A chameleon. But I got to thinking that most, maybe all animals are camouflaged in some way. Lions are the color of dust and dry grass, good for sneaking up on zebras. Snakes you hardly see among the twigs and roots until you nearly step on them. They're made to fit their environment. It protects them against predators.

"I'm thinking all these thoughts, in my cell, when I look at my own skin. It doesn't match the concrete walls or steel bars. And this voice asks me, 'And what environment are you made for?' Man, you know the voice when it hits you. It wasn't strong, wasn't thunder and lightning. It was true and it hit right where it needed to hit. It hits you like the gavel, convicts you. God was not inviting me to speculate on this or draw up imaginary worlds like a child. This was a real question, a life-and-death question. A real gird-your-loins moment.

"The question contained the answer. I don't know how else to say it. Like hidden in code, subliminal. It was there in the speaking. That's when it all clicked. This skin, these eyes, these legs standing me upright, this tongue, all of it is made to praise God in *His* world, in *His* natural environment. My whole life suddenly made sense and all that those good people were trying to do. This skin is going to glow in the glory of God.

"That's the camouflage. I'm already wearing it. It was

just a matter of time to find the right place to watch it glow. That's why I signed up for Project Abel when I heard about it. Man, I begged. People pretended there was no such project, even some of the very same people we saw at the warehouse that day. Finally, this chaplain comes to see me. Has an owl-head cane, like he had come straight from God, right on the path of my prayer. Asks me some tough questions. I told him what I just told you. Told him my life isn't about this life, and if I could do something with it other than rotting away in a prison cell for forty more years, I would do it, even if it meant a cruel and unusual death."

"Like being crushed to death between two planets?" I said.

"Even then, Shelton."

"That same chaplain came to me," I said.

We lay for a while longer and reorganized the day. Launce pulled the deck of cards out of his pocket and flicked toward the river all but the four aces. There were no more hours in the day, just unequal lengths of time: before the eclipse, the eclipse, after the eclipse. And as we came closer to Gogmagog, the day itself looked more and more like one long night.

27

What we did measure were the hours and minutes between tremors, like the contractions of a woman about to give birth. There was no hospital to which to race. There was no midwife waiting around. Instead, we explored the length of the Royal River. For the other guys, who were convinced we were going to die, the trip was about enjoying one last bit of life. For me, it was about taking a look at the dull gray rock the Lady had convinced me was about to turn into gold.

The grasses, reeds, and flowers we had sown lined the banks for miles. There were bare patches, where the rock was hard, but wherever the river bent and left sand and silt, the green stuff grew. It took a day, but we flew the length of the river until we arrived at a large lake. This was a beautiful spot, a broad valley surrounded by tall, craggy mountains on one side and soft white cliffs on the other. I was imagining building a small hut for myself to live in when Launce staked his own claim.

"Man," he said, "I could ride out the end of the world right here. Or, if people do come, picture it: tall pine trees at the base of those mountains, tall grass in between. We'll get old Doris to send us some deer to hunt, finally get a little meat in our bellies. A little fish, too. We spend the day farming and fishing. That's a life. I can see it all, right here. Hell, why don't we just stay?"

The memory of Mireille's neck flashed in my mind, the golden morning sunlight playing on the hairs of her neck. I remembered the dream I'd had at some point on this trip, of the green trees in front of the white church and the dark landscape beyond. That had been a wedding, one I had hoped would have been with Mireille. She was not here and would never be, not if we crashed into Gogmagog. Yet, this was the place about which I had dreamt. These white cliffs were my church.

"I say we stay here, too," I said.

"That's two against two," Launce said.

"Fellas, if it's meant to be, it's meant to be, and we'll all get back here," Prosper said.

"It's really any hour now," Bel said. "Look at the horizon."

The outer edge of Gogmagog was about to sink below the horizon, in every direction. Soon there would be no more sunlight on Lapis Elpis. This was the darkness I had dreamt, the barren world in front of the white church. Maybe what had felt like a wedding was my funeral.

We took a shortcut back to Valley of the Kings, a direct line from the lake over a few ridges. We made it just on time. It was night, I knew, because Gogmagog was almost fully aglow. The rumblings were ongoing, some barely fading out before others came up. Sometimes the ground shook, like in an earthquake. One violent quake knocked me off a rung of the ladder coming out of my cell and sent me back down with searing pain in my ribs. I worried that I had broken them all again and had to sit in my seat for an hour after taking some aspirin. At one point during that hour, the shaking was so violent that I took the Ardeen a few feet off the ground for some relief. When I set us down again, the other guys took down the dome tent so we could fly off at a moment's notice. They had been hollering about something, and with the tent out of the way, I could look upward and see it for myself.

Big Red, a thousand miles away, had erupted. A tongue of thick black cloud licked the horizon. The plume had to have shot into space for us to see it from so far.

"Not space," Bel said. "Let's keep our heads. The plume is simply traveling toward us on a jet stream. By the look of things, that's all of Big Red. I bet the entire volcano, all sixty-six thousand feet of it, burst into dust."

"Yeah, that's keeping our heads, Bel," I said.

The earthquakes did not stop. Bel had the bright idea of inflating the hull to give us some cushion. We decided to sit on the upper deck of the can and watch while the world around us turned to dust.

During the long night, I spied another red glow on the horizon. This one was much closer and clearer than Big Red. A volcano had grown right out of the flat rock a few dozen miles north of us. It sprayed lava high into the blue-green night, and a glowing red river ran off to the east. I warned the guys.

"Man, I hope it doesn't clog up the Royal," Launce said. "This is a good river."

A few hours later, another volcano erupted, not far away to the west.

"Any chance this gets over all at once?" I said. "I don't want to suffer. Or suffocate."

"We could wait it out at sea," Launce said.

"It's days more back there," Bel said. "And we'd only be prolonging the inevitable. And blinding ourself to it. I want to see what hits us."

"No, gentlemen, this is it," Prosper said. "We make our final stand here."

Lapis Elpis had gone from the quietest place I had known since the death house, perhaps in all the universe, to nothing but light and noise—low, distant rumblings and nearby claps of thunder from clouds formed by volcanic dust.

I had known the procedure for my execution, had it memorized down to the minute. Time had belonged to me. This world had been one new threat of death after another, all of which we had passed through pretty easily. We might go out sucking in Gogmagog's own gas in a few more hours, or a crack could open in the ground a few minutes from now. But I wondered to myself if the Lady or Huntsman or either warden or the priest with the owl-head cane, anyone, would come and tell us it was over, that we had passed this test, we had sent the signal, Lapis Elpis was a failure, and we were being sent back to prison. I knew about guys who had committed crimes once they were out of prison just so they could go back to a world where things had been more certain, where they knew how to operate, where they had a place.

All the time in the world, Bel had said. There was very little time left in this world. Gogmagog filled the night sky. I made out finer details in his gas clouds, intricate swirls and swirls within swirls. Fractal geometry, Bel called it, and no one answered him because there was little left to say. We could only watch—contemplate, as Prosper called it—the beauty of celestial death.

***

Day came, and day meant night. Gogmagog blocked our two suns, and the day was going to be one long eclipse. Day and night had reversed, and what we had for day now was the glowing night of Gogmagog.

The Royal River drew down into a trickle. Some lava flow or deep fissure had blocked it upstream. Our perch on a hill inside a bend of the river had left us safe from the worst of what was going on—except the dusty air, which made work of every breath. Prosper would sing, stop to cough, and keep going. Launce accompanied him on the electronic guitar the computer had. I lay flat on my back on the upper deck of the can most of the time, waiting for the final blow: a scalding piece of rock thrown from a volcano, a crack opening to the molten center of this moon, Gogmagog's blue-green stench suffocating us. It was growing hot outside, and the air was hard to breathe, but none of us wanted to spend our last minutes in a cell.

At glowing night again, the ground shook with an earthquake, but the module, on the inflatable hull, did not shake entirely with it. We floated and bounced a bit before settling down again a few inches from where we had started.

"Now explain that," I said, still lying on my back, to whoever would listen.

"I wonder if our two gravities are balancing out," Bel

said, also lying down. "This is the part where Gogmagog really takes over. The next bounce could take us all the way up, all the way in."

"It has begun," Prosper said. He was somewhere outside the module.

For all of Prosper's solemnity, I sat up and looked around with the same nonchalance I'd had the morning of my execution. "Can't we tie this thing down? I read that somewhere once."

"We sure can," Launce said. "Come on. If we deflate the hull, we can tie down from the bottom rim of the fuselage, hammer tent spikes into whatever cracks we can find."

Prosper, Bel, and I moved slowly. Part of it was a sudden lack of interest in doing anything to survive our obvious doom. Part of it was no longer having a good grip on the world below us.

"It's like we're walking on the moon," I said with a bundle of rope in my hand.

"We are walking on a moon," Bel said, taking the rope from me.

"No, I mean the real moon, like in the old days, before the moon became whatever took us here. Hey, maybe our two moons are related, like sister moons, you know, how they have sister cities?"

"I do not know what a sister city is," Launce said from underneath the module, where he tied lengths of rope to hooks on the bottom rim of the Ardeen.

"You know, like they have on the old welcome signs: *Welcome to Rochester, New York. Sister City with Bamako, Mali.*"

"You're suddenly calm," Bel said.

"Prosper said it. It has begun. What's there to worry about?"

The guys were not calm, I could tell, so I kept quiet and started hammering a spike into a crack in the ground. What hurt were not the downward thrusts but keeping the heavy hammer from hurling backward when I pulled it up. Gogmagog was trying to take my tools.

Once we were tied down and Launce tugged all the ropes to make sure they would not come loose, we stood around and waited. Every step I took risked bouncing me above the Ardeen. We still shook while lying down on top of the Ardeen, so I lay down underneath it, under my cell, with my head poking out to see the action above. Prosper lay down near me, under his cell, and put his hands behind his head. Bel tossed ration wafers next to us.

"For the moment itself, so we can cross the Styx."

"I've had enough of this food for one life. I don't want to eat it in the next," I said.

Bel and Launce lay down on the other side of the can. The four of us lay there for a few minutes, which was all the time in the world Bel thought we had left.

The ropes tightened, and my body rose gently against the underside of the module. Gogmagog was sucking us in. It was midnight, and the planet was fully lit—except where our double shadow, the one made by our two suns, filled its center. We were going to pass through our own shadow. That was my strange new hope, to pass through the shadow of two suns into another world.

Beyond a sky full of ash I could see lightning shoot

across the atmosphere. I could not tell if it belonged to Lapis Elpis, Gogmagog, or both, like static discharge from finger to doorknob. The sound was ours, thunder followed by sizzling, as if the sky was on fire. We were entering Gogmagog's atmosphere, or as Bel specified during his commentary, its ionosphere. At least I would know where I was at all times. This was the new procedure for my execution: death by planetary gas chamber.

"Yes, sir," Prosper said. To whom, I did not know.

I looked over.

Prosper had pulled himself from underneath the Ardeen. I turned to see him squatting and holding onto the bottom rim of the can. He shuffled away from it, enough to clear his knees.

"Prosper, what are you doing?"

"Gird your loins, Shelton. This ride ain't over yet. We're gonna keep on creating this world."

"What?" I said when Prosper thrust himself upward. I watched his muscular body soar upward. He spread his arms wide. He became a silhouette against the ashen blue-green sky and soon disappeared into its folds.

I kept watching and noticed that the lightning stopped. I waited for the moment, the great conflagration, and it did not come. After a few minutes, the rope slackened. The rumbling of the ground continued, and the legs of the module began to scrape back and forth against the rock. I looked past my feet at Launce. He tossed a Hidden Rat into the air, and it fell again, slowly. I pulled myself from underneath the can and stood up. Still holding my hands to the side of the module in case I slid upward again, I looked up and around.

Gogmagog still filled the whole sky, from horizon to horizon. Then, it did not.

"Yo, guys," I called. "Check it out. Look east."

On the eastern horizon, a thin black line grew thicker. Soon, stars appeared, the brightest ones that could shine through the thick smoke. Launce, Bel, and I stood along the Ardeen, gripping its sides, while we watched the universe unfold in front of us. Above and behind us, to the west, Gogmagog peeled away. It took a few hours, but soon the whole night sky was ours. We did not say much, still expecting some disaster, some final blow to knock us down. It did not come.

"Now, what?" I said.

The two suns rose. Lapis Elpis was a heaping mess, a house an animal had rummaged through. Volcanoes were pluming everywhere. The sky was full of smoke. The Royal River was dry and some of the grass had burned. We untied the Ardeen and took it upward to have a broader look. It only took a few minutes to find Prosper.

He had fallen back to the ground about half a mile away. His arms were still spread wide, and he had, at least I thought, a slight smile on his face. His body was not mangled or smashed, which told Bel he had fallen softly on the return to Lapis Elpis and might have died from smoke inhalation hundreds of feet in the air, where I had last seen him. I placed a Hidden Rat in his mouth.

"Tell us what you see, Prosper," I said.

"Bel, what happened?" Launce said.

"We skipped out of Gogmagog's orbit."

"At the same moment Prosper pushed off?"

"He said this ride isn't over," I said.

"No, it's not," Bel said. "Might be a stay of execution. We could be spiraling deeper into space, away from the suns."

"No," I said. "He did it."

"Okay, Shelton," Bel said and patted my back.

28

"I don't want to bury him here, where there's no water," Launce said.

"But the other guys are here," I said.

"*Were* here," Bel said. "Based on how much time it looks like has passed since then, the way this place twists time, they might be only bones. If that."

"Let's take him to the lake," Launce said. "Let's start over there."

"That's downriver," Bel said. "It'll be dry, too."

Launce pursed his mouth and looked toward the horizon.

I said, "What did Prosper say? 'If it's meant to be, we'll all get back there.' We survived two planets smashing against each other. I can't think of a better sign that it's meant to be."

We sat Prosper in the vestibule where Sal and Cricket had sat and Ash and Willand before them. Prosper had no partner in death. Maybe the man had killed Gogmagog.

We took the shortcut, cutting across the many bends of the Royal River, back to the lake and its valley, which we had not yet named. We arrived before sunset. The place seemed fine, with no active lava flows. The lake was still filled, but the water was tainted with ash. The tall, rugged mountains in the distance were different—some of their peaks had sheared off and left immense vertical walls. The white cliffs had not fared much better, but the crumbling chalk had revealed a cave a hundred feet or so up the rocky slope.

"You see?" Launce said. "God wants us here. Carved a home for us."

Bel rolled his eyes.

"Yeah, well, I hope God sends us some new air soon," I said. I rubbed my fingers together. "The ash is falling. And it's getting cold again."

We buried Prosper on the lake shore. Between Launce, Bel, and me, no one knew what to say. Launce finally started.

"Lord, receive Prosper Us. He was a positive man. He spoke of you. We will miss him. May we prosper in his absence. Amen."

"Amen," I said, and I sprinkled seed over his grave.

"Amen," Bel said and also sprinkled.

The ground rumbled.

"Alright," Launce said. "We start again."

"Start what?" Bel said. "Nothing's going to grow under this ash. I say we wait it out for a while. We've got years of rations. We hole up in those caves."

I said, "Yo, I'm not going in there while the ground's still rumbling."

"Me, neither," Launce said. "That chalk'll bury us alive and its dust choke us in the process."

We put the Ardeen on a low rise, far from falling rock, far from rising tides. Days passed. They were thirty-six hours long, eighteen of ashen sunshine and eighteen of choking, freezing night. It was too cold to sleep anywhere except our cells. The lake began to freeze over. Gogmagog pulled farther and farther away. Our only consolation was that the days were still growing shorter by about a minute at each sunrise.

"Why is that a consolation to you guys?" Launce said.

I said, "Because it means we're creeping up on a normal Earth day again. Like Bel said, we're making this planet to fit us."

Bel said, "In any case, it means change. Shorter nights, maybe warmer days. A target, if you will. Something to look forward to."

Launce said, "Change could always be for the worse. Let's keep busy. I've got to do something."

The tremors and earthquakes became less frequent, so we set to work outside the chalk caves, chipping away to make bricks to build a windbreak around the Ardeen. The computer had warned us a couple of times about the reactor overheating, working too hard against the cold outside, so we had to keep the temperature down inside. My shivering bones clacked against each other at night. But the bricks kept breaking apart under our picks. The chalk turned hard and glossy too quickly for us to shape the chunks into proper bricks. When we tried to saw through them, we had to break the blocks over our knees to free the saw again. Finally, Launce suggested we open up the biggest cave to receive the Ardeen. It took days, but we succeeded in carving out a vault just big enough for the can. In this situation, it actually helped that whatever kind of chalk this was, it hardened when exposed to air.

During this time, something took root around Prosper's body. Mushrooms and fungi. They would survive our volcanic winter. No one dared eat a mushroom.

I said, in the direction of Prosper's grave, "What do you say, old man? You put in a good word for us with the Big Guy or what?"

A few hours later, I was drawing in my cell when small shadows started creeping across the page of my sketchbook. They were snowflakes, big ones.

"Great," Launce said. "Just what we need."

"Yes," I said. "Exactly what we need. Snow means it'll get warmer. Trust me on this. I know winter."

"Hey," Bel said. He was collecting the flakes in his hand and rubbing his hands together. "It also means no ash. The snow's pulling the ash out of the sky."

We waited. The heavy snow fell like footsteps, an army against the ash. After an hour, the wind picked up and made a frenzied battle.

"That'll do it," Launce said. He went inside the Ardeen and lay back in his seat.

I found a place just inside the entrance to our cave where the wind was not lashing at my face, and I watched. A drift formed at my boots. I was warm inside, and all the warmer for watching the cold outside. I thought of Mireille, but the thought did not stick like it had used to. I thought of the New York collectors, the ones who had set me up to sell their drugs. My chest burned with anger, but the fire soon faded. We collectors had prided ourselves on weathering the long winter to bring an old world back to life. We had rummaged through abandoned houses, offices, and museums, places everyone had passed over. We had found freedom in our lives by picking alone through the past, measuring what we had found against the value those in a new world might give it. The people who had moved south and to the Sahara had been making a new world since the Merge. I could hold nothing against them for that. But they could not hold a candle to this storm, to the snow scrubbing a brand new sky of smoke and ash of a planetary near-collision. If and when people ever came here after me, it would be just that—after *me*. After burying four of my brothers and seeding the world with them. It might be a million years before Lapis Elpis ever was habitable by humans, and I would be long gone by then, but every yard of soft, grassy soil they put beneath their feet would be me. All my anger left—anger at the stupid life my mother had made for herself and me, anger at Mireille for never really wanting me except to make herself feel bigger, anger at my own stupidity with the New York guys I should have always known never wanted my good. Anger gave a man reasons to fight for his own life. He would find things to be angry about just so he could live. The ash in the air was the violence of this planet—it was its own planet now—pulling away from its fate. Lapis Elpis had been angry and had won her justice, her freedom to fly around her two suns on her terms. The snow was here, in crystalline beauty, rational wisdom, to clean up after that anger. Lapis Elpis had fought for her own life and won. Looking out at her, I had no more anger, nothing more for which to fight. This was her battle, perhaps had always been her battle, and the other guys and me her pawns. I was hers. On Earth, I had never been what someone else's anger had tried to protect. In the arms of Lapis Elpis, I was the possession of her anger. That meant life for me. Life would mean I had once been here, and always would be, in one form or another. What that chaplain with the owl cane had seen in me was true. He had seen my truth before I could. I wanted life, and life wanted me. It had taken a whole new world to make me see it.

It snowed, on and off, for weeks.

***

Almost a month after the Near Merge, our almost-collision with Gogmagog, I woke up to a blinding white sunrise. It had finally stopped snowing, and the clouds and ash had cleared. Fat Man had found a gap in the distant mountains, and his spreading rays bounced off the thick blanket of snow covering everything in Prosperous Valley and reached deep into the chalk walls of our cave. The light on Lapis Elpis had never been so bright, and I searched for sunglasses in my trunk. My whole world had become white and turquoise. Only the most vertical parts of the distant mountains rose gray through the snow.

"Well," Launce said, stretching his lanky arms. "About time we see what's out there."

It took a few tries to clear the six-foot snow drift blocking our way out of the cave. The module wanted to bounce upward with each strike against the snow, and this risked denting the upper ring of the can against the chalk lintel of the cave opening, to say nothing of sending the cave crumbling back down upon us. "Small steps" became our mantra.

But it was big steps once we were free. We made longer hops with fewer bodies weighing down the Ardeen. First, we went back to Valley of the Kings and found it also covered in snow. From there, we would retrace our steps, all the way back to the coast.

Clearwater Crater was lightly ringed, all around, with the trees we had seeded. There were patches of forest on its side and along the streams flowing from its base.

"Man," was all Launce could say. He knocked snow off the branches of a young pine.

"Winter wonderland," Bel said. "It worked here, too."

"This is even more impressive than the grass," I said.

"Yeah," Bel said. "Yeah. Way more impressive. Too impressive. This is years of growth, not months."

I hung like a monkey from a branch. My ribs had healed. "What are you saying?"

"You saw all the grass at Valley of the Kings. I'm saying that time is passing more quickly for the plants than for us."

"Or things just grow faster here," Launce said. "We gave them good fertilizer. Powerful poo."

"But we didn't lay down our dung everywhere," I said. "They've spread beyond it. Same with the grass at the graves. That went all downriver. I hear what Bel is saying. Something more is going on here. This place is gold, like the Lady said."

"How can time pass more quickly for one creature than another?" Launce said.

"I'm sure the Lady knows," I said.

No one answered.

We flew on. The base of Sunset Cliffs was no longer a safe spot to land, so we landed above and hiked down to

Pine Groove. The rock had broken and fallen away. One lone pine tree stood where we had first planted.

"Not quite," I said, leaning against the trunk of the tree. "Look down."

We had come from behind and did not see, until I leaned against the tree, what had become of the rest of Pine Groove. Low trees, tall bushes, and bright grass clung with gnarly fingers to every crack and gap in the rocks for hundreds of feet down the slope. There were even dead trees lying on the ground, already rotting and no good for firewood.

"Man," Launce said. "Would you look at that."

"That's us," Bel said. "We did that."

"I don't know," I said. "I mean, yeah, that is us, like clinging to the rock for dear life and finding it. What I would say though is, you think all this would have happened, taken root, if the rock hadn't fallen? We just had some shallow grooves before. Now it's…look at it. The earthquakes gave the plants something to cling to. It all had to happen this way."

For reasons I did not understand, my eyes started misting over. I plucked pine needles from the tree I had been leaning on.

We decided to stay through sunset, in honor of our first visit here and the trees we had made grow since then. There were no clouds this time, just a clear view out to sea several miles away. At sunset, Fat Man and Little Boy took their turns dancing red and gold on the endless breakers.

When twilight blue finally gave way to black, Gogmagog appeared just above the western horizon, about the size of Little Boy and still glowing blue and green with traces of gold. It was not bright enough to keep out our stars. We had a whole sky filled with stars, thousands of them.

"Myriad," Bel said.

"A plethora," Launce said.

"Multitudinous," Bel said.

"Innumerable," Launce said.

"You think one of them is the sun?" I said.

After a pause, Launce said, "We'd have no way of knowing. No way of mapping our way home."

"This is home," I said. "Where our brothers are buried. Where we'll be buried."

"Still," Bel said. "It would be nice to know where to look."

"Hey," Launce said, "but the IOSS is supposed to find us. We're supposed to send a signal."

"What signal?" I said. "The can doesn't even have a radio."

"Did we plant a maple tree somewhere?" Bel said. "Imagine the first homegrown food we get is maple syrup."

"Put that on a Hidden Rat," Launce said.

"Not a bad idea, actually. God, I'm tired of living like a vegan."

"Wait a minute," I said, and I pulled from my pocket the pine needles I had plucked. "We've got it right here. Pine needle tea."

That night, the three of us drank pine needle tea, the first food we had grown on Lapis Elpis.

Our next hop, the following morning, took us to Stairway to Heaven. But the tall, narrow canyon that had led us to Stairway from the sea was much wider and shallower now. Its steep, noble sides had crumbled. The veins of lapis lazuli for which we had named this planet had disappeared beneath the dust and snow. Stairway, too, was almost an island between the two broad rivers whose convergence it had once marked. We followed the canyon out to sea.

Either the sea had risen or the whole continent had fallen, close to eight thousand feet.

"Or both," Bel said. "Because why not both?"

"One way to tell," Launce said.

We floated on the sea to take depth readings. The ocean, which had been a consistent four hundred feet deep during our time, was now between six and seven thousand feet deep. The sea had risen, and the land had sunk.

"Alright, I've got a theory of my own," I said. "Y'all listening?"

The three of us were still at sea, sitting on the edges of our hatches, drinking more pine needle tea. Bel stuck out his hand to tell me to go ahead. Launce seemed indifferent.

"It is this, my brothers: time is moving faster for things with less life in them. It's like the reverse of life on Earth. We change the slowest because we have the most life in us. The plants are changing faster than us, growing up and dying before we can turn around again. The rocks are changing faster than them. I mean, think about it: all this rock forming, us colliding with a planet, how long does that take in real time? A thousand years? That's cosmic time we've experienced in just a few months."

"For which geologic time is a blink of an eye," Bel said.

"We could be centuries old by now," I said.

Launce wiped his mouth. "Millennia."

"Eons," Bel said.

"Meaning, Earth and the IOSS could be a distant memory," I said.

No one said anything because we all knew the implications of that. The only person I thought of was Dr. Huntsman, the last woman I had seen on Earth. I had spoken offhandedly, without weighing the implications of whole eons of history on this planet—and Earth—passing by with every breath we took. She and everyone else would be dust by now.

We followed the canyon and its river inland as far as it would take us. After a few days, we arrived back at Prosperous Valley. The Royal River, which we had once crossed by chance on our way toward the center of the continent, turned out to be the same river by which we had first breeched the continent.

"Everything looks the same as we left it," I said. "Snow and everything."

"There was a lot of snow," Bel said.

"So much for my time theory."

We kept going. We arrived after a few days at Big Red. Nearly leveled to the ground, it had become the broken rim of a deep blue lake twenty miles in diameter. Outside the rim was a vast plain of black, hardened lava.

"I wonder if Degory made it out," Bel said.

"Notice you didn't say, 'I *hope* Degory made it out,'" I said.

"I said what I said."

We went on for weeks. We mapped the entire continent. It was, for the most part, circular in shape, with some island chains running out to sea. It spanned twenty degrees south to twenty degrees north, and the same east to west, as best we could tell, forty-nine hundred miles in diameter. At about six million square miles, it was the size of Antarctica and even more circular in shape. Most of it looked the same, homogenous as Bel called it, gray rock covered in black volcanic sand and snow drifts filthy with ash. There were no great mountain ranges, just a few series of still-active volcanoes and the system of concentric ridges of varying height, which collected the melting snow into lakes and small rivers. There were some big rivers like the Royal. Many canyons broke through the steep coast, the way the edges of a cookie crack when they cool after being taken out of the oven. We called the continent Watchman's Eye, since this had been the part of Lapis Elpis that was always facing Gogmagog. We planted trees, grass, and flowers in a few choice places.

One reality on which we kept our own watchman's eye were signs of the separation of the continent. The massive tidal forces of the Near Merge and the explosion of Big Red had ripped the Watchman's Eye into six unequal pie slices. In places, the fault lines were a few feet wide, in other places, just jagged hairline cracks. But they grew bigger the longer we traveled, which told us that geologic time really was moving quickly. The canyons at sea's edge were the end of those fault lines. The world might have six new continents before any of us died of old age.

Someone else had also been working quickly while we were surveying the continent, and that was Prosper. When we returned to Prosperous Valley, his dead body had made the place true to its name. The snow had mostly melted, leaving behind a thick mat of ferns and funguses. Grasses and flowers had come downriver from Valley of the Kings. The volcanic ash might have been choking us before the snow, but now it was our soil, soil that Prosper, in his rest, had been tilling and strengthening until we came back.

29

Launce, Bel, and I started right to work at preparing the land in Prosperous Valley to receive real crops. We had high-density rations for years, just in case our crops failed. Our dead brothers had left us their supply. We did not want to chop down the trees we had to make fire, not yet, and we could not cook with the near-boiling water out of the taps in our cells, which had been hot enough just for making coffee and pine needle tea. So, we had to pick crops to grow that we could eat, more or less, raw. Launce thought he could devise a kind of Dutch oven to fit underneath a hover engine, but those engines generated more electrical burn than real heat. So, we settled on fruit, nuts, vegetables, and grains like oats and quinoa that, when ground, cooked enough in the briefly hot water for us to chew. In the meantime, we would live off the tree nuts, peanuts, squash, and carrots in the beds of deeper soil we had piled up.

"Man, I haven't worked like this in years," Launce said after a few days. He put his hands on his hips and stretched backward. "I'm whooped."

"I've never worked like this," Bel said. He stayed bent over a garden row, leaning his arms on his knees.

"Me neither," I said. I smacked a bug against my neck.

The day had quickened to just over thirty hours, fifteen of daylight and fifteen of dark. It had been easy enough to stay awake during the day, but we were still having trouble figuring out what to do with the extra hours of dark we did not need. We never argued when someone wanted a nap because all three of us were putting in the effort.

"I honestly thought we'd be fighting monsters or hacking through alien jungles," Bel said. "I never considered taking the IOSS seriously when they said we'd be the first living things here. We've spent months just sitting in our cells, hovering around. Maybe we should've been doing this kind of work from the beginning. We got soft."

"Monday morning quarterback," Launce said. "We had no idea what we were facing. We did the best it seemed to do. Besides, how could we have tilled the soil before there was any soil?"

I swatted at another bug. "Y'all notice the bugs are getting worse since we landed?"

"Yep," Launce said.

Bel stood up straight and looked around. "Bugs."

"I don't even know what they are. Little gray things," I said.

"Bugs," Bel said.

"Bugs," I repeated, trying to figure out what Bel had in mind.

"Did we have bugs before?" he said.

"Before when?"

"At any time on this trip."

I pulled my head back. "Bugs."

"Bugs," Bel said, nodding.

"Hey," Launce said. "Bugs."

"We've got bugs," Bel said. "We're not the only animals on this planet anymore. Their eggs must've come inside some seed packets."

"Or stowaways in our gear," Launce said. "Or someone's hair."

"Bugs aren't animals," I said. "I'm glad we've got company, but I wish it were real animals, like cats and dogs. Maybe some birds to eat these bugs. And a cow, to get some steak. And a milkshake."

"Bugs are animals," Bel said. "Look it up."

"Alright, while you're arguing about this, I'm going to lay me down a while," Launce said. He walked up the chalk cliff to a smaller cave he had claimed as his bedroom, where he had set up his pup tent and trunk. "Bugs."

"What about you, Bel?"

He sighed. "I'm getting there myself. But I think I'll refill the water in the Ardeen from the lake first. Did you clean out the filter last time like I asked?"

"Yes, Dad."

Bel took the Ardeen to the middle of the lake, which had swelled from the snowmelt. I worked on for twenty minutes and saw him still out there. He was taking a nap, I was sure, letting the gentle waves lull him to sleep.

A solitary cloud covered Fat Man, leaving me chilly. When it did not pass, I put on my winter jacket. Turning around to do this, seeing the cliffs and garden in shadow, left a sense of dread in me. Everything was so quiet. Bel was asleep in the middle of the lake. Launce was asleep in his cave. I was alone. For the first time since the flash flood, I was out of reach of anyone who could help me if something went wrong.

I ignored this feeling as long as I could, and another twenty minutes passed. It nagged, though, this irrational fear. I heard Launce walk around, rustle in his tent, and cough strangely. The cloud passed and left me in sunshine again, but the fear remained. Finally, I chucked a stone in the lake, hoping Bel would hear the splashing. His cell was on the other side of the can. "Bel," I called.

Something was wrong. I walked up to Launce's cave to see what we might have to do to intervene. I did not want to swim in the chilly water just find another dead body in the can, if that was the case.

When I was halfway up the path to our caves, where the path began to slope down again, I saw Degory walk out of Launce's cave. He wiped something from his mouth. I froze. He was disfigured—the skin on half of his face looked like melted plastic, and burnt winter clothes clung to his skin. Through the burnt half of his face, a bloody red eye stared menacingly at me. Through the tattoos on the healthy side of his face, a clear blue eye gazed at me serenely. I swallowed to clear my throat for speaking, but my brain would give me no words. It was not Launce I had heard walking before, but Degory. He had probably pounced on Launce through his pup tent. The cough had been Launce's only reaction to being stabbed.

Launce was dead, and Degory had been eating him. It was blood he had wiped from his mouth. I knew that because Degory still had the knife in his hand. If he were innocent, he would smile, put his hands up, do anything he could without a tongue to reassure me. He did not. Instead, he started walking toward me.

With more calm than I had ever known, I pulled the knife from my coat pocket and unfolded it. Degory stopped. His clear blue eye was calculating his next move. His red eye wanted to pounce on me, but his blue eye held him back. He pinched his lips. I was a volcano, ready to blow. I could feel the lava rising. But a heavy weight held me back, as if the air had formed a hand and wrapped it around me. This would not be like with me and the cop. I had the uphill advantage. I had the same knife as Degory. I had been better fed, more rested. And I was no longer naive about Degory. I would be in the right.

I held his eyes. He might try to hypnotize me with his snake eyes, but it would not matter. Not for long. I forced down a smile. He could not see what I began to see out of the corner of my eye. But a word tore at me. Finally, when the time was right, I said it: "Checkmate."

Bel slammed the Ardeen against Degory, knocking him against the cliff wall and onto the path. I ran down, and without a second's hesitation, I stabbed Degory in the stomach repeatedly. He struggled upward until blood spurted from his mouth. His burnt ear had been toward the lake, and he had not heard the whirr of the module's engines. He had not seen the bishop coming in across the long diagonal of the chessboard. When he stopped moving, I knelt on the arm that held his knife and cut his throat. His blood ran down the path, toward the caves. I stood over him, knife in hand, nostrils flaring, and the volcano erupted. I screamed at him. Drool ran from my mouth. I looked up and howled.

I turned to find Bel and invite him into the howl. He had landed the module at the base of the cliff, not up by the cave. He slowly climbed the ladder of his cell and fell on his butt on the upper deck. He leaned to one side, then to the other, and with his free hand, he held his heart.

"Oh no. No no no no."

I ran down the path to him. At what point I put the knife away, I did not know. I flew through the vestibule like a cat across a tree limb and into my cell, where I tore apart my cabinet looking for aspirin.

"Shelton," he said weakly.

"I'm looking."

"Shelton."

He did not want aspirin. He wanted me.

I sat next to Bel, on the edge of the hatch into his cell. I tried opening the aspirin bottle, but he took my hand and held it very firmly. I put my other arm around him.

"We got him, Bel. He's dead."

"I pushed her down." He spoke in a whisper. "She was nagging. All I did was push a little. Her head hit the edge of the dresser."

"You're alright now, Bel, you hear me?"

"I stood over her and said, 'Congratulations. Now I'm the idiot you always thought I was.'"

"I'll tell you what you are, Bel. We built this crew around you. I waited to ride with you. You showed up, first thing, defended us all. You fronted all those scientists. I got Sal to come along. Launce, too. Did you know one of the IOSS people had asked him to wait for the last module? Did he ever tell you that? So he could apply his piloting skills to us. They thought we had the best chance. Because we were smart and skeptical, the last in line. The last shall be first, like Prosper always said of us. Module Nine. Here we are, Bel, because of you. None of us could've done it without you. Look around you. All this life, this world. A whole planet is alive because of Bel Chichacott."

He nodded. I pressed my mouth to the top of his head.

"And of all the crew, Bel," my mouth tore back angrily against my tears, "you're the most like a father to me. Taught me so much. Made me a man."

Bel's hand relaxed. I held him for a long time.

***

Daylight was running short. I laid Bel on the upper deck of the module. I put Launce and Degory in body bags and put them in the vestibule so I could ferry them down near Prosper's grave. I had to dig this time. These were the first graves I'd had to dig in the ground instead of pushing away sand and piling up loose rocks. The rocks in Prosperous Valley had been covered by the soil, which was a foot thick with volcanic ash and fungus fibers. It was not hard to shovel away, but I did have to do it and move more from elsewhere to cover the bodies. Chunks of chalk from where we had cleared the path and opened the caves would have to do for covering them at least today. By sunset, I could barely lift my arms. Three pairs of boots were still exposed. I covered their feet with my own body bag; there would be no one to put me inside of it.

From left to right, I had Bel, Prosper, Degory, and Launce. I had thought about dumping Degory into a volcano, or far out at sea, or in the sulfur spring, which was probably no longer there after the Near Merge and all its upheavals. But if he was going to eat Launce—and he really had started to—I was going to eat whatever his skinny body fed into the soil and into my garden. The hazel trees were sprouting. Lapis Elpis made quick work of plants. I would eat real food again soon.

"Enough of this," I said out loud. I leaned my head and hands on the end of the shovel. "Think real thoughts now."

I leaned my chin on my hands and looked at the graves. I straightened up and said, "Alright, God. Here they are. Bel, Launce, and Degory. I know they're sorry for their crimes. Bel said so at the end. In his own way. I don't know much about Degory. Or Launce, neither, what they did. I never looked it up."

I gazed across the lake.

"Why didn't he just stay with us? What did he think he was going to get from this world by going off without us? We'd all four of us still be here."

I used the shovel to fix a corner of the body bag covering their boots.

"I don't know what else I'm supposed to say. I don't have Prosper's songs, or Launce's. I just want to honor them, my brothers, my fathers."

I heard the sound of something being set down by the caves. I turned around, but nothing was there. It could have been Launce's tent flapping in the breeze.

"Best I can do is name things, God. I don't have real

prayers or nothing. So, here it is. This is what I do. If you're gonna stick me here alone, I'm naming everything my way, and you're gonna respect that. This lake is Bel Lago, after Bellarmine Chichacott. This valley is Prosperous Valley, after Prosper Us. The caves are A Worthy Place, named for Launce Holsworthy. I should name something for Degory. Maybe what's left of Big Red. Big Rodriguez. I don't know. I'll think of something. But it'll be mine. If you're even listening."

I started to turn around and said, "That's all I've got. I'm all alone now."

My shoulders started heaving, and my whole body shook. I pounded the shovel against the ground.

"Is this what you want? Anything else you gotta prove?"

It took a few minutes of tears to formulate another word.

"I'm all alone. Like I've always been. And I'm hungry. I'm so damn hungry."

All at once, my tears left. Fat Man had set, and Little Boy was an hour behind. It would be dim blue light until it set. I finished shoveling dirt on the body bag to cover the feet of what remained of my crew.

When I was done, I saw Gogmagog rising above the distant mountains. It was barely bigger than a star now but very bright and green.

I took the Ardeen into the large cave and set it down. Nights were still chilly and, being all alone, I wanted to sleep locked in my cell. I compromised and put up the dome tent. I locked the vestibule door, the only way in.

***

I slept through the night, or most of it. The deaths of three men did not take any more time off the day. That had been Gogmagog's work, primordial time.

After a breakfast of a Hidden Rat and bad coffee, I set out for the garden. The best way to honor my brothers would be to make this land give life. It might be just me, but I had to hold out hope, which I defined as measured expectations based on a promise, the promise that the mysterious signal would be sent to the IOSS and people would come here to live. No matter how much time seemed to pass on Lapis Elpis.

As I walked by Launce's cave, I heard a funny noise. I brought a flashlight from the module and shined it around. I looked across the garden at the gravesite—none of the bodies had budged. I shook the slashed remains of Launce's tent and tossed it outside. The noise was coming from his trunk. I dragged it outside. With my knife in one hand, I pried it open with my boot. Degory could have left the statue of an Aztec god inside, and who knew what kind of demon would come flying out. Nothing flew out. There were bugs inside, though, big ones. I leaned forward. They were bees.

"Lady, did you—?" I began to ask when I felt the urge to count them. There were eight bees, seven workers and one queen. The seven were for my fallen brothers. I wondered where my bee was when I felt the urge to look out over the garden. I nodded. "Get to work, Shelton Keyes. Busy bee."

30

Nine years passed. Those were nine Lapis Elpis years of six hundred eleven days. The days had slowed to twenty-seven hours, over all that time. All told, that made seventeen Earth years. I was less and less certain, though, that days and years marked time at all. It was simple motion around two suns. Time was the way they controlled you in prison. Here, everything moved free. So did I. You could call nine years like this your own solitary confinement, but I could go wherever I wanted, and watching a new world come into being, I did not feel alone. Lapis Elpis had become my sister and her children—the plants, the bugs, the bees—my friends.

Only by the movement of the two suns around each other did I even know what a year was. There were no seasons on Lapis Elpis, at least not the way seasons happened on Earth, with the changing angle of Earth to the sun giving longer and hotter days or nights. I figured we had first landed when Little Boy was lined up perfectly behind Fat Man, and I called that New Year's Day. Over the course of the year, Fat Man and Little Boy flew apart and came back together, so much that for parts of the year I was left only with Little

Boy's dim blue light for hours at a time. Those were miserable months.

There were no months, though, not really. Lapis Elpis had no moon of her own, not that I had seen, but over the years several thousand meteors had burned up in the atmosphere applying for the job. A few had struck hard enough for me to feel. So, I divided six hundred eleven into twenty months of thirty days and made a special month of eleven days around the new year. Each month was five weeks of six days. I did not need a sabbath day. I knew what Prosper would say, but being busy every day kept me from thinking about being alone on my own planet.

There were no other planets I could find except Gogmagog. I always knew where Gogmagog was in the night sky.

Nine years passed, and Lapis Elpis had become a living planet. Only the obvious places, like fields of hardened lava at the center of the world, the sand deserts of the southeast, and the steepest and highest rocks, were not covered in forests, bushes, grass, or at least ferns and moss. The wind had done most of the work. The bees had been busy playing catchup with the flowers and fruit trees, which had kept mostly to my slice of Watchman's Eye, the name we had once come up with for the continent.

Watchman's Eye was now six distinct landmasses, though, spreading away from the center, from Big Rodriguez, pretty quickly. The landmass I called home—though all of Lapis Elpis was mine—I called Ardeenia, after Module Nine. It was where my crew had spent most of our time together. It was a rough triangle of a continent, a knife blade, pressing westward. As it pushed its way, it did all the things continents do, like creating mountains. Ardeenia had a real mountain range on the west coast, with snow-capped peaks and everything. Sunset Cliffs were long gone.

Over nine years of fast-forwarded geologic time, a lot changed in Ardeenia. The Royal River dug a canyon, and the canyon filled up with silt. Then the Royal shifted somewhere else. Bel Lago's shores eventually ate away at the four graves on its shore, my first garden, and a big chunk of the chalk caves of A Worthy Place. I had to work quickly to carve deeper into the chalk. Then, the waters pulled back and left Bel Lago just a river. Floods and fires came from time to time and destroyed much of my work but not all of it. Diseases ate away at a lot of what I had planted but not all of it. Volcanoes spewed ash in the air, but it settled again. Earthquakes ripped away at Ardeenia but could not tear it apart.

When the first corn crop had come in, a few weeks after the last deaths, I had done something an outside observer might construe as religious. I still had no firewood, so I roasted seven ears of corn under one of the Ardeen's engines. This did not make them edible. Instead, I tossed them, one by one, into the Royal River. I spoke the names of my brothers as I did: Sal Combes, First to Go; Cricket St. Clair, Eagle Eyes (he had first spied land and had always been looking at me); Randall Chudleigh, Gogmagog's Own Son; Prosper Us, God's Own Son; Launce Holsworthy, Man of Honest Mistakes; Degory Rodriguez, Man of Molten Rock; Bel Chichacott, the Bishop. After these seven, I tossed an un-roasted ear of corn in the river and said, "Shelton Keyes, Not Yet Ready."

That had been nine years ago. At thirty years of age—

or thirty-eight, Earth time—I was not sure I was ready yet. Someone, however, thought I was.

One sunny noon during the first part of the year, I sat in my cave home eating a lunch of beans, rice, and okra. Footsteps came up the path. They were slow and steady, with no prominent heel strike. I continued eating even though butterflies had taken flight in my stomach. I thought the Lady was back. She stopped well before the entrance to my cave. I set down my bowl, stood up, and walked over to my footlocker. Inside was the second orange jumpsuit the IOSS had given me. I made it my dress suit for such an occasion—my first jumpsuit was filthy.

I walked into the light of a turquoise sky and saw a tall, serious man standing thirty feet down the path. It was not the Lady. He wore a long, loose black robe and had fancy sandals on his feet. He reminded me of the priest who had come to visit me in the death house but walked without a cane. I opened my hands in reluctant welcome. He walked forward. His eyes were deep emerald green, and they seemed to glow. He was very tall, taller even than Randall, who was six-foot-six, but thin like Launce, lanky-strong. His face was like that of the priest I had seen, old without wrinkles, almost ageless.

"Welcome to Lapis Elpis," I said.

"Thank you." He had a slight accent.

"Are you God?"

"Hardly."

"Are you the devil?"

"I came close once."

"Are you the Grim Reaper?"

THE SHADOW OF TWO SUNS

"No. I have only swung my sickle once."

"I get it. You're a convict, too."

"You are wise, son."

"What are you in for?"

"Murder," he said.

"Death penalty?"

"Plea bargain for a life sentence. Or you could say the sentence was commuted."

"You a part of Project Abel?"

"I've been doing this a lot longer than that. You might even say Project Abel was my brainchild."

"Y'all get the signal?"

"Yes."

"What was it?"

"The chirping of a cricket."

"A cricket? Are you saying…what are you saying? Was Cricket an inside man?"

"I'd call him the ringer. The man committed a lot of crimes but probably not the one for which he had been sentenced to death. He died here. That was the signal."

"That an innocent man died here?"

"I would not say an 'innocent man.' No one has been innocent since the beginning. It's more like blood spilled unjustly cries out to heaven. One simply has to be listening."

"You're welcome here and all, so I mean no disrespect, but would you talk straight? What's your name?"

"Qayin."

"Kai what?"

"Adamson. But you people know me as Cain."

Lightning shot through my stomach. A man from the

Bible was here. I did not know what kind of judgment this was going to be. Or what fresh insanity I had sunk into.

"May I come in?" he said.

I turned to look at the home I had made. "Where are you taking me?"

"Nowhere, Shelton." He cleared his throat. "On the contrary. I'm sending people to you."

Nine years. The signal had arrived. It had been Cricket all along. Or at least when Randall had killed him.

"Come on in," I said.

Cain, as the man called himself, studied my parlor. From the glossy white walls of oxidized chalk hung useful pieces of the Ardeen: vinyl seats, polyester tents, nylon ropes, aluminum screws and panels, rubber gaskets, and plexiglass windows. The rusted metal hull would not come apart, so I left it with the spent rod of plutonium in its reactor on a dry hilltop. My bed was an inflatable life raft I had found in the module, turned upside down.

"Would you care for some lunch?"

"Just some tea, if you have it."

I boiled water over a wood fire. After nine years, I had acquired a hefty wood pile.

"What is this?" Cain said, pointing at the drawings I had hung on the wall.

"It's silverpoint. Drawings made by scratching metal into chalk. I ran out of pencils years ago."

Cain looked at me the way Bel would sometimes, like he already knew what silverpoint was.

"Anyway, it's our story. A graphic novel, if you will. Each frame tells a scene in the foundation of this planet: assembly on Atlantis, the trip through the portal, four days in space, and so on."

"Atlantis?"

"That's what we called it. It fit the bill: middle of the Atlantic ocean, clay pots and stone buildings, portals to new planets. Is it not the lost city of Atlantis?"

He turned to study my panels. "You people need a better definition of the word 'city.'"

I remembered the vision the Lady had shown me, of a universe at peace, a million golden worlds at one.

"Did you come through the same portal?" I said.

"Not exactly. And I certainly did not spend four days in space, like you did. No wonder Doris couldn't track you."

I checked the boiling water and held back a smile. "Did she find the other crews? Didn't they go through space, too?"

"I saw most of the signals right away. One group of self-proclaimed gladiators had been having a particularly good time."

"Wait a minute. If the signal was unjust execution, are you saying that the whole Project Abel was built on the chance of one of us being wrongly convicted?"

I poured hot tea into the heavy plastic cups left over from Module Nine.

Cain smiled. "I admit, it was a game of roulette. But there's always a bullet in the chamber. There always has been. Hence, Project Abel." He sipped.

"I'm sorry, I don't get it."

Cain smiled again. "Tell me your story first. And take your time."

We sat down. I had set up two chairs from the module,

side by side, where I normally ate. A full dining room would have made me lonelier. The extra chair had always been for this occasion. I told him my story.

Cain said, "Do you really believe that Prosper pushed Lapis Elpis away from Gogmagog with his jump?"

"Let me put it this way: I know that a man weighs nothing compared to a planet. I also know, because Bel repeated it often, that correlation is not causation. But if I had to choose, I would not risk Prosper not doing it. He died, but he knew what he was doing. Maybe God does speak to people, and Prosper was convinced of something in that moment. And here we are. Where are we, exactly?"

"You want coordinates? Those I cannot give you because I did not arrive here by them. Nor will anyone else."

"Then how did you get here?"

"Let's just say you're within walking distance of Eden." Cain smiled and sipped his tea. "A long walk."

I leaned forward and put my head in my hands. "Sir, I truly do not understand who you are and why you're here."

"If it's any consolation, Mr. Keyes, neither do the people who sent you here."

"Then how did they do it?"

"They saw a door, and they walked through it. That's the way we have been doing it for millennia. Only this time the door has taken you to another state of the universe."

"Another state? Yeah, things were pretty basic when we got here."

"Elemental, you might say, based on your story. Just like Earth was when my father arrived. Bel was on to something with his theory."

I leaned forward and stared into my tea. "Listen, I've got to ask you, being who you are and all: am I dead? Did I actually get executed?"

With great gravity, Cain said, "Do you feel dead? Don't you trust your own body, your own reality enough to think you'd know the difference?"

"Well, like I told someone else, someone else who appeared to me just like you, I'm not sure I ever really felt alive before. Not until I buried Launce and Bel, anyway. I know people feel less alive after they lose someone. I guess I felt that way after my mother died. But it's different now."

"Because you probably felt nothing much before you came here, nothing but dull anger at a world you did not understand. We're more alike than you realize."

"Is that the real reason you sent death-row inmates to settle new planets? 'Cause they're like you?"

Cain closed his eyes and leaned his head back.

I tapped the empty teacup on my leg. "You want to know something? The first time I killed, it was because I wanted to die. The second time I killed, it was because I wanted to live."

The man kept his eyes closed. This allowed me to study him. He breathed, and his muscles twitched. There was nothing about him that said he was unreal, a hallucination.

"So, what's the next step?" I said. "How do we get people here? When do I see what the Lady showed me?"

He turned his head lazily, in a way that did not match his solemn bearing. "If the Lady showed you something, that's for you. But I'm glad you mentioned it." He faced forward again. "It proves my point about you. Doris wasn't going to go for you."

"She came up to me before I boarded. The only one she did that to. I thought it was because she liked me in a certain way."

"She was studying you. Wanted to see what I had seen."

I sat back in my chair and sighed. "Women, man. The guys ragged on me the whole time about that."

Cain stood up. He gazed at me with those glowing green eyes. "There is a lot she cannot see from her side of the abyss."

I stood up. "Abyss? I mean, is this it, the end, am I going to hell?"

He put his arm around my shoulder. "Let's go outside."

I pushed his arm off. "Look, man, just maybe let me set things right first."

He walked outside, turned around, and spread his arms wide. "Come, look at the world you've made, Shelton Keyes." He bowed and motioned me forward.

I stood next to him, looking over the garden and the lake.

Cain said, "Does this look like judgment to you?"

"I mean, you're the bad guy, right?"

"I'm a murderer. So are you. Read my story again, the sentence I was given. And ask yourself: do you feel like the bad guy, especially when you gaze across the beautiful world you and your fellow criminals have made?"

I had no answer. If I had not done what I had done, I would be struggling to survive on a hostile Earth. Instead, I had prepared a whole new planet for people to call home.

"Ask yourself other questions, Shelton. How does a world transform so fast? How does Cain get here? How do *you* get here?"

"I took a submarine through a portal at the bottom of the ocean."

"And passed through space. *Deep calleth upon deep.* Now ask yourself on which side of the Flood you're on, which state of the universe you're living in."

"That is too much for me, sir."

"Yet, here you are. When the others do come, you won't speak with them the way we are doing now. They won't see you the way you saw your brothers. You will be a shadow they will never see but you will shape a world in which they can prosper. They'll never know what you're doing for them and even if they try to deduce your presence you'll remain a glint of light they'll only suspect exists—a specter, you might say. You'll be standing watch, patrolling a new world, protecting it from elements in this universe that want to stop life before it really starts."

"You make me sound like a cop."

Cain grabbed my shoulders, pressed his forehead to mine, and said, "Now you understand true justice, Shelton Keyes, and what it can accomplish."

By the time I recovered from this, I saw Cain disappear over a distant hill.

***

I did not know when to expect people to arrive, but it would not be right away. Cain had come for me, not for them. To shake off the wild thoughts I was having, I did what had become my favorite thing; I rowed the life raft to the ocean. The Royal River was broad and calm, a perfect place to contemplate.

After a few weeks, I passed through the mountains guarding the way to the sea. A few stone walls I had built on the beach served as a hut. I took off my boots and stood where the gentle waves washed over my feet.

One wave passed, but something remained on my foot. The seas had been glowing with algae for many years, but when I looked down, I saw a thick piece of clear slime. Another wave washed over my feet, but the slime remained. I poked at it with my finger. It flashed bright purple and ran off. Another one, just like it, scampered out of the waves onto my foot then followed the other one. I watched the two creatures, the first real animals I had ever seen on Lapis Elpis, chase each other along the surf.

"Ash, Willand, it's good to see you again."

I looked up. A dark line traced an arc from horizon to horizon, centered on Little Boy. It grew thicker, like those first spirals of fire had when we had arrived. Coils grew around it, just like before, but instead of fire, the coils were like sparkling blue electricity. They pulsed downward in both directions from Little Boy, well beyond the northern and southern horizons.

This went on for two and a half days, seventy hours. When it ended, I knew this world was no longer my own. But whoever they were, they would live here thanks to me and my crew.

* * *

ACKNOWLEDGEMENTS

Thanks, as ever, to Danielle Dyal of Bookfox. She cuts away all that is not living from these books.

A warm appreciation to the people of Corpus Christi and Notre Dame, my home on Morningside Heights.

And to my family, whose love has nurtured this work from the beginning—especially my father, Tom, who has been these books' biggest champion.

The quotation on the dedication page is from the following: Calvino, Italo. "The Origin of Birds." *The Complete Cosmicomics*, Mariner Books, 2015, pp. 170.

Milton Keynes UK
Ingram Content Group UK Ltd.
UKHW041310061224
3480UKWH00015B/30/J